Letters from Brackham Wood

(A Moira Edwards Mystery)

by

Rita Gard Seedorf and Margaret Albi Verhoef

For information, email **Cozy Cat Press**, cozycatpress@aol.com or visit our website at:
www.cozycatpress.com

COZY CAT
P R E S S

ISBN: 978-1-939816-34-4
Printed in the United States of America

Cover design and Digital Manipulation by Anita B. Carroll
www.Race-Point.com/

1 2 3 4 5 6 7 8 9 10

We dedicate this book to our children: Scott Michael Seedorf, Anna Seedorf Bollinger, Gretchen Verhoef Wanzenried and to our grandchildren: Roselyn Mae Wanzenried, Benjamin Henry Rose, and Alexander Thomas Rose.

Acknowledgments

Thanks given— For their historical perspective of the World War II years: *Jeanne LaLone Ager, Betty Harrington, William D. Roberts*, and *Jennine Darlow.* For facilitating interviews: *Molly Roberts Hannan and Kathleen Reilly Imholt.* For previewing the manuscript and generously giving their sage opinion: *Anna Seedorf Bollinger, Jeff Bollinger, Judy Crabb, Jennine Darlow, Mary Daugharty, David and Marcia Gifford, Jennine Murphy, Kerry Moxcey, Joyce* and *Bob Sleeth, Gretchen Eileen Verhoef, and Susan Whitman.* For their patience, love, and support, our husbands: *Martin Seedorf* and *Douglas Verhoef.* To *Martin Seedorf, retired EWU Professor of British History*, for hours of individual instruction on "World War II in Great Britain," and endless pots of coffee! And, of course, to *Patricia Rockwell* and the Cozy Cat Press.

Prologue

Writers must write. I have done so all my life, never thinking of what would happen if I were forced to stop. Six weeks ago, I was felled by a spectacular and public accident while ice-skating on a pond designed by the Olmstead Brothers in Manito (pronounced MAN i toe) Park in the small city of Spokane, Washington. My disposition must have suffered from being sidelined by one broken leg and one broken arm because my usually good-humored wife shoved a large tin box into my lap and commanded: "See what you can do with these!"

She timed her command perfectly. I was trapped. With both my left arm and left leg in casts, getting up out of my chair was a major undertaking and was impossible with a large box on my lap.

My resentment vanished as I began to read. The box held sixty-four letters written between cousins Moira and Margaret: the first mailed in 1937 and the last in 1944. I found myself swept into the current of their lives during those precarious years. The letters portray more than the growth in the relationship between the two women. They reveal the differences between the worlds of Moira in England and Margaret in America, differences that became even more pronounced after England declared war on Germany in 1939.

I know history. I studied it, lived it, wrote it and used it to interpret my world. I know about leaders and wars and innovations. I have a grasp of chronology and geography and the shifting sands of leaders and movements and physical boundaries. My knowledge even spreads to the reality of daily life in Europe and America.

However, these letters humbled me. I realized that I know less than half of history: the history of the male. What were women doing as the men of Hannibal's Army crossed the Alps on elephants? What was life like for those who stayed home keeping children fed while facing privation, destruction, and fear? How did they repeatedly cope with decisions that they had no part in making? Extraordinary though they were, these bright articulate women spent their lives dealing with not only the world I know so much about but with another world that I can only imagine.

I could write much more about these two women, but I will cede the pages to their own words.

****

January 5, 1937

Dear Cousin Margaret,

You will no doubt be surprised to hear from me after so many years. I am certain that you remember the fond times we had playing together when we were very young children. Unfortunately, I lost track of you in the turmoil that took over my life after my parents died.

After they passed away, I was unable to find an address for you. I have recently moved to a new household and, as I was unpacking, was surprised and delighted to find the address where you and your family lived many years ago. I had tucked it into a small pocket in the handkerchief sachet that I have carried with me for nearly twenty years. I have no memory of putting it there.

I write in hopes that this letter will eventually reach you. There is much to tell you and I will be happy to do so if, indeed, you are still at this same address.

With this letter ride my hopes that we will be able to make contact once again. You and your parents, should they still be alive, are my only living relatives on this earth.

Sincerely,

Moira Edwards

*****

February 18, 1937

My Dear Moira,

How wonderful it was to hear from you after all these years. I am utterly amazed, as I had all but given up hope of ever seeing you or your dear parents again. I can't bear to think they are lost to us.

Your letter was delivered to Mummy and Father's address. They still live in Chicago in the same house they bought in 1912. They added two bedrooms shortly before 1919. I think they thought that you and your parents would join us some day and that you would stay with us until you found your own home. Father updated his skills by taking classes at Northwestern University Medical School. He then took a position there as a professor. He also worked at Cook County Hospital. Mummy managed the house.

Mummy forwarded the letter to me and both of my parents are now anxiously awaiting your news. They will be devastated to learn of your dear

parents' passing. My parents have aged, but they are very much alive and pleased to be grandparents. Mummy's cousin, Gillian, lives with them and helps with chores that Mummy can no longer do.

I have so much more to tell you, but shall keep some of the happenings of the past years for future correspondence. I will tell you, however, that you have four relatives other than Mummy, Father, and me: my dear husband, Charles Walker, our two boys, Willy (William) and Bert (Robert) and our daughter, Catherine.

I no longer live in Chicago, but in a small, but fast growing city in the state of Washington. It is called Spokane. When next you write, my address is 207 West 14th Avenue.

Charles is a journalist following in the footsteps of his father and older brother Thomas. He works for our newspaper and is assigned to the international scene. We do take pause at the stories from Germany. I hope he is never sent there to cover what is happening.

We met during college at Northwestern. I was fortunate to have Father teaching there, as my tuition was waived by his work. I, too, became a doctor. In another couple of years, I hope to go to work full time, but currently I work two days a week in a Women's Clinic. I am a general practitioner.

When I am not at the Clinic, I care for our children and I belong to a Ladies' Auxiliary. Our knitting committee just completed making caps for the American Red Cross and our sewing committee is making layettes. The volunteer work is not what I want to do forever, but it is very worthy work as there are so many in need of assistance.

What do you mean you recently moved to a "new household"? Do you no longer live in your parents' home? Surely you completed school and went on to follow your dreams!

Oh! Do write soon and tell me everything.

Fondly,

Margaret

*****

March 15, 1937

Dearest Margaret,

Can you imagine the joy that I felt when I received your letter? I sat holding the sealed envelope in my hands for an hour before I slit it open. I was cherishing the realization that I was not alone in the world. Opening it to find out that not only are you and your parents alive but that you have given birth to Willy, Bert and Catherine. It was overwhelming. How I would love to meet all of you and your dear Charles as well. Even though that is impossible, our contact with one another is gift enough.

I am gratified to know that you have from time to time thought of me and wondered about my fate as I have yours. It is a comfort to discover that you are happily married and living in Spokane, Washington, and that dear Uncle Basil and Aunt Elizabeth are alive and remain settled in Chicago.

Had I not been orphaned when my parents died in the 1919 influenza pandemic, I imagine that my life would be very different from the one I now live. I love learning and had intended to one day become a teacher of English Literature in a girls' grammar school. I was a happy day student at Charwell School for Girls when both my parents were struck by their fatal illness.

Mother, Father and I were very close and, therefore, until they passed away I had never realized that we led an isolated life. Mother was an only child and Father's only sibling was your father, Basil. As you may remember, we spent all holidays and many weekends together before your parents immigrated to America. I often overheard Mother and Father talking of joining you. Father was ready to go but Mother was hesitant. All such speculation ended when our country entered the Great War in August of 1914. When the war ended four years later, they had begun to discuss it once again. However, the influenza epidemic soon reached our area and they both fell ill. They passed away within the same week.

My parents had sacrificed to pay the tuition that allowed me to attend grammar school. Therefore, when I lost them, I not only became an orphan, but without resources to pay, I was forced to leave my school at the end of the term. I said goodbye to my parents, my classmates and my dreams within a very short time span.

The teachers at my school treated me with great compassion at that time. During the weeks between my loss and the end of the school term, Miss Grey, my Maths teacher, took me to live with her in the small flat she shared with her aging mother. My History teacher, Miss Henderson, whose mother had recently died, took care of the many details that naturally occur at such a time: service and burial, the selling of our household goods, and I am sure many other duties of which I was unaware.

I was 14 years of age when my parents died and, since the school leaving age was 14, I was able to secure a situation which supplied me with room and board. Miss Smith, the head mistress of Charwell School, compassionately found me a position with her close friends and I became a mother's helper with the Mayview family, who understood my circumstances. I will always be grateful. They treated me as a member of their own family as I worked through the grief of losing both my parents and my planned future at the same time.

During the nearly two decades that have passed since that time, I have held positions in many households and always happily moved on to the next family. I am confiding in you as I have in no one else when I tell you that just prior to taking my current position I began to work toward a new goal. I have determined that I will one day own a bookshop. To prepare myself, I began reading during the few free minutes between the end of my workday and my much needed sleep. In my last position with the Barrett family, I was allowed to borrow books from the family library. Since I have moved to my new position I have been making good use of Cooke's Free Circulating Library. Frugal living has enabled me to begin saving a few pounds that I trust will one day allow me to purchase my shop. My latest position allows me much more time to read and to add to my account at the Brackham Wood Building Society. Yet I find myself uncomfortable about my present employers. I will write more of it in my next letter.

I look forward to hearing more about your family and your life in Spokane, Washington.

Your loving cousin,
Moira

*****

June 1, 1937

Dear Moira,

The postman just arrived with your latest letter. It is wonderful to have found you again. Even though it means that we can only dream of seeing one another, it is most exciting waiting for the mail.

I suppose it is unproductive to even wonder what your life might have been, had you and Aunt Jane and Uncle Reggie followed us to the United States. Nonetheless, it disturbs me.

I have spoken with Father and Mother, telling them that you are alive and well. Your parents' demise distressed them immensely. However, the sadness they feel is far outweighed by the fact that you, who were once lost, are found again.

Now I must tell you something about our life. Spokane has a population of about 140,000 people and is located on a river, which cuts it into two sections. We live south of the river, but when I go to the Clinic, I travel to the city's north side. While my work there is primarily pre-natal and child welfare, I also see women. There are so many who were affected by the Depression and have no means of paying for their care that most of our work is done at no cost to the patient. We do get some assistance from community funding. Many parents bring their children to the Clinic fearing they have the dreaded polio disease. I fear for my own children as well. It has become an epidemic in the United States. Even our President Roosevelt has not escaped it.

I call our home a *Heidi* house. Do you remember reading that wonderful book? I call it thus, as it resembles how I imagined Heidi's home. The house was designed by an Easterner, (that's what we call someone who originally lived on the east coast of the United States), named Kirtland Cutter.

Our home is not a mansion, but it is a cozy replica of a Swiss chalet. It is constructed of dark timber and has a lovely basalt wall surrounding the property. Basalt, a type of rock, is plentiful on this side of the river and because of this, is used in many homes and gardens.

You are a very resourceful woman, saving funds for the bookshop of your dreams. It is most admirable. I hope you write more of your plans. Each of your former positions has brought you closer to that dream. You are not unlike our Amelia Earhart and her dream to fly around the world. We women must keep our dreams alive by never giving up the challenge set before us. Charles is covering her story, with trepidation. It is highly unlikely that she will ever be found.

Your discomfort with your current employers makes me uncomfortable. The fact that you did not tell me more has left me on pins and needles. Do remain watchful of this situation.

Lovingly,
Margaret

*****

July 20, 1937

Dear Cousin Margaret,

What joy to hear of your three children and your life in America. I am thrilled and amazed to hear that you have studied medicine and are now a physician and am proud that you are providing medical assistance to those who are less fortunate.

We in England also have been in reduced economic circumstances. In truth, our country has never recovered financially after the Great War. Until we began our correspondence, I had no one with whom to discuss news in the outside world. Other maids-of-all-work, with whom I briefly converse as we go about our shopping, are not the least bit interested in anything beyond their daily lives and sharing the gossip from households in which they work. Many of them are able to talk freely with the woman of the house but I am denied that companionship by the taciturn nature of Mrs. Malthorpe.

From your description of your lovely home I conclude that it would have few equals in the village of Brackham Wood where I have lived as of late. The majority of houses here are of a simple two-up two-down design, with two reception rooms down and two bedrooms up. Most two-up two-downs are terraced houses; rows of mirrored or identical fronted houses connected by common walls.

The Malthorpe home, where I currently work, is designed in much the same way but is a detached house with a narrow garden on each side. The rooms are a bit larger and light can enter the house from all four directions.

I am both amused and encouraged by your comparison of me with Amelia Earhart. I have not such an adventurous spirit. However, an English woman with aspirations above her station, even if they are kept secret, is quite brave in a way. Since I read your comparison, I have been following her adventures even more closely. Therefore I was devastated last evening when I heard a news report on the wireless reporting that the search for her aeroplane had been abandoned.

But I must try to explain my discomfort with my current position. I now realize that it actually began during the interview. First, I must give you a little background on my job history.

During Victorian times, the term 'maid-of-all-work' was the lowest of all servants save the scullery maid. However, in this part of England, the title now refers to a helper to the woman of the house, usually as the single servant. Modern conveniences, such as water piped to the inside of the house and electric lighting have made housework easier. At first, as with the Mayviews, I worked for board and room. By age 22, I had enough experience to be hired for pay and became a proper maid-of-all-work. I found work easily and have never found it necessary to present my application to Miss Packham's Placement Service.

However, the position I am now holding came to me quite differently. Out of the blue I received a letter from a Mr. George Malthorpe of Brackham Wood asking me to meet with him regarding a position in his house. He made no mention of how he had come upon my name. I thought the request strange because I had never before been contacted directly by a future employer. At first I hesitated. However, since the Barrett family, for whom I had been working happily for two years, was about to immigrate to Canada, I saw no harm in chatting with him.

I returned his letter and we arranged to meet at Cole's Tea Shop. I was to recognize him by his brown overcoat and he was to look for a woman with a blue hat and black coat. I was ill at ease for the first few minutes of the meeting. It had always been the lady of the house who had spoken to me about the household duties.

He asked nothing about my previous experience or my housekeeping skills and did not ask to see the letters of reference that I had with me. He questioned me only about my family and background. I told him of the untimely death of both of my parents in 1919. When he pressed me about other relatives, I told him that there was only you, my cousin Margaret, with whom I had lost contact many years before.

Once he was satisfied that I was unencumbered by family, he offered me the position. Only then did he disclose the duties and the rate of pay that he was offering. Whether or not he knew it, he offered me twice the pay and half the work of any of my previous positions. Perhaps it was my bookshop dream that caused me to override my reservations and accept the position on the spot.

Since the postman is about to arrive I will describe my duties in the next letter.

Lovingly,
Your Cousin Moira

*****

August 25, 1937

My Dearest Moira,

I have told you little of my life in America and how I came to live in Spokane. I will endeavor to put some of those years on paper.

Charles and I married in 1926, after our graduation from college. He was fortunate to get a position with the *Chicago Times*, where he had held various jobs since beginning undergraduate school. I

entered Northwestern Medical School, which became four years of struggle. We had very little money and what we did have was used for my books, transportation, and daily living. The fact that Father taught at Northwestern University meant that my tuition was compensated and that became a huge advantage especially when the Crash occurred.

We were able to live with Mummy and Father in their extra rooms which helped immensely monetarily although it gave us very little privacy. I would cook and clean during the few free hours I had. Any extra money was given to my parents to help with the running of the house. I suppose I should be grateful and not complain that I became pregnant. Were it not for Mummy caring for the baby during the day, and Father advocating for me in medical school, I would have had to leave school to care for William. By the time I graduated, I was pregnant again with Robert but managed to hide my growing body.

All the hospitals to which I applied denied me a Residency because of my gender. By December of my final year, I was so depressed that I became convinced that I would never achieve my dream of following Father in Medicine: all because of being a woman.

But I had given up too soon! Charles' older brother, Thomas, had moved to Spokane in 1926. He suggested that I apply at Sacred Heart Hospital, a growing Institution, which had been established here in 1886. I did apply and thankfully so, as I was accepted. I believe that perhaps the West Coast is somewhat more enlightened than the rest of the country; or at the very least, less discriminating! Charles is a wonderful husband. I am ever so grateful for his support of my dreams. Not all men would allow their wives the opportunities that he has allowed me.

I can't tell you that all my male peers are confident in a woman's ability to practice medicine. I am one of only a few women practicing in Spokane. Only one of us has a private practice. This experience has alerted me to the plight of women in a man's world. I feel great satisfaction working in the Women's Clinic.

I sense adventure and intrigue in your latest position with the Malthorpes, Moira. Why ever would you be hired without being asked for your references? I think that I would be concerned about Mr. Malthorpe's interest in your lack of family ties! Why would that be so important to him? Do be careful!!

On the other hand, I can barely contain my excitement, awaiting the description of the duties he expects you to perform. I can't imagine what you could be asked to do, in light of your employers not knowing anything of your capabilities.

With love,
Your Cousin Margaret

*****

September 15, 1937

Dear Margaret,

How delightful to receive your letter and hear of your life. Communicating with you has changed my life. Finally, there is someone in whom I can confide. Your reflections on my life and description of yours give me a new vantage point. And I love hearing about dear Uncle Basil and Aunt Elizabeth. How did our parents lose contact after being so close? I suppose it happened during the war. Much was disrupted during that time. Speaking of letters, I just read that in America the Post Office delivers the mail while here in England the Royal Mail delivers the post. I am certain that we will discover many other differences between American English and the language spoken here.

Your warning to be careful has motivated me to apply for a post office box at the postal counter located in Green's Grocery and Dry Goods. Trustworthy Mrs. Grey, the proprietress, has promised to pass your letters to me only when there are no prying eyes. I will send you my new mailing address when I am approved and assigned a box number. I am always the person who sorts the incoming post in the Malthorpe home, but I would still prefer to have my own private box, if only to protect you, my dear cousin. You will remember that at my interview I told Mr. Malthorpe that I had lost touch with my only living relative.

When Mr. Malthorpe hired me, he had recently married and was soon to move into Michelsgrove, his childhood home, with his bride Harriet. My duties were to cook the meals, keep the house, and do the mending. He made it quite clear that there would be no children to mind and that he and his wife, Harriet, rarely entertained at home. When he added that my salary would be twice what I was now making and that the laundry would be sent out, I was astounded. Compared with the requirements of other maid-of-all-work positions, this situation was most appealing.

I met Mrs. Malthorpe the day that we all three moved into Michelsgrove. We found it furnished exactly as it had been when George Malthorpe was a child. A tatty green overstuffed chair and settee filled the front room and, in the bedrooms, knotted ropes tied to the bedsteads provided a base for lumpy mattresses. The kitchen was primitive except for the addition of running water and a pipe that drained the used water through the wall to the outside. The flush toilet was three yards down the back garden in its own brick house. After I scoured and organized the kitchen surfaces and gave the rest of the house a good cleaning, the place was very livable.

During the past two years, the overstuffed chair and settee have been reupholstered in a muted flower pattern and a proper outside drainpipe has been fitted to the kitchen sink. The beds were also modernized. The woven ropes that supported the lumpy mattresses have been replaced by box springs and the local upholsterer re-stuffed the mattresses and covered them with strong new fabric. These changes made the home quite comfortable.

However, the most welcome change for me was the installation of a flush toilet in a small alcove at the rear of the house, which is entered through a door cut through the outside wall of the house allowing one to reach the lav without going outside. Many homes now have toilet rooms attached to the house that cannot be entered without going outside. Those who live in such homes must still walk out the back door and a take a few steps to reach the outside door of the lav. On a dry summer day that extra walk is no trouble. However, during a rainstorm or the winter months, I am most thankful for the renovation.

Upstairs, the bathroom, which contains only the bathtub, was modernized by the addition of a new geyser that heats the water in only two hours. The old one took five or more hours to generate enough hot water to fill the huge tub.

Life is very easy for me here in contrast with my old positions in busy households with children running at my feet as I kept the house tidy and the laundry washed and ironed and often cooked the meals as well.

I have ample time to read and am constantly borrowing new books from the library. At first I was thrilled to be working toward my goal with both my learning and my savings account. But after a time, I began to notice how different our household is from others, though from the perspective of an outsider, it looks like a typical childless English family.

My curiosity about Mrs. Malthorpe grows daily. She is barely a mistress to me. She behaves as though she has never before supervised a housemaid. She has no interest in planning meals and eats whatever is put before her without complaining. In fact, she takes scant interest in food. In general, she pays no notice of anything that goes on in the house. Her mind always seems to be on something else. I cannot make sense of her behavior.

In a later letter I will describe the duties of a more typical maid-of-all-work position and you will understand why I took this job despite my reservations.

I am very concerned about the Italian dictator Mussolini, whose troops have been in Ethiopia since 1935, the German dictator Adolph Hitler, who reoccupied the Rhineland in violation of the Treaty of Versailles signed at the end of the Great War and General Franco, who declared Spain a dictatorship. I remain concerned even though our new Prime Minister, Neville Chamberlain, who recently took office, assures us that all is well.

Please give my best regards to your Charles and your parents and a hug to the children from 'Auntie' Moira.

Lovingly,
Moira

*****

October 1, 1937

My Dear Moira,
Indeed our two languages have some strange words. A "geyser" in a bathroom would most definitely be unheard of in this country. The only geysers I know of here are in Yellowstone National Park in Wyoming. One geyser is named "Old Faithful," as it spews boiling water from a hole in the ground at regular intervals. Can you imagine hot water being hurled into the air at heights of more than 100 feet? Some eruptions have even gone as high as 185 feet. Although I have never seen the sight myself, many tourists find this attraction most interesting.

We are fortunate to have water—both hot and cold—in our kitchen and bathrooms with a mere turn of a spigot. Seemingly endless hot water from a pipe is especially welcome on the days we do laundry! The best news about doing laundry though is the latest model of washer which has the entire mechanism enclosed. We are hoping to have enough money saved by next year to purchase one. I worry so about getting my hand caught in the wringer, but with the new machine there will be no worry as the washer spins the water from the clothes inside the tub.

Thank heavens you now have a post office box! At the very least we will have privacy in the exchange of our letters! How dare the Malthorpes read your mail! It would be suspicious though for you to receive any sort of mail I suppose, considering how the man repeatedly asked you about "living relatives."

I must say that your description of Mrs. Malthorpe sounds most strange. Do you suppose some malaise affects her? Her lack of interest in her home and meals makes me suspect depression. Perhaps, as you suggest, she has no knowledge of running a household. If that be the case, then no wonder she has no interest!

I'm being somewhat forward in asking, but do you think that she is happy in her marriage to Mr. Malthorpe? My dear Moira, in America, we are known to be somewhat unconcerned about others' sensibilities, so I apologize if I have offended you; but what if he is a cruel miscreant? What if she was forced into a loveless marriage?

One of my appointments at the Clinic this week was a young woman, Sarah by name, who had a simple rash. The patient seemed to want to talk and spoke English quite well. I listened and I learned that she, along with her parents and sisters, came to our country from Germany about six months ago. I do not know what brought the family to Spokane, but the father is a baker and, although he does not have a shop of his own, is baking in their kitchen and selling the breads and pastries from their living room! He must not have been able to find local work to support the family.

We not only treat the ailing, but our volunteers attempt to aid patients in other ways, such as finding them lodging, jobs, clothing and the like. Sarah needs work and we hope to find her a position as a nanny. Although, she appears to be very

capable with the children, there is something that preoccupies her. If she is to become a nanny, the children she cares for must have her undivided attention. I may have more to tell you about her in another letter.

With love and curiosity,
Margaret

*****

October 10, 1937

My Dearest Margaret,

I enjoyed reading your last letter. Your worthy work at the Clinic sounds so interesting and impressive; going beyond medical assistance to help in other ways. You must meet a broad spectrum of people. I imagine that immigrants from other countries also come to you for help. I am curious about Sarah and what worries her. We English are more reserved and try very hard not to reveal our preoccupations or worries. We are raised to 'keep a stiff upper lip.' In this country, if one threatens to become discouraged, one is told to 'keep your pecker up.'

I have seen a picture of the geyser in the Wyoming part of your country and heard it described on the wireless. At first I didn't recognize the word because Americans pronounce it with a long "I" sound while we pronounce it 'geezer.' I never tire of learning American English and how it differs from ours.

Our new geyser is a huge hot water tank attached to the wall at the tap end of the tub. A careful balance of scalding hot water from the hot tap and water from the cold tap provides me with a luxurious weekly bath. Since there is no automatic shut off valve, we must all three be very careful to shut off the geyser once we fill the tub.

From this explanation of our hot water system, you will understand why I was so pleased to take a position in a household where the laundry is sent out. It is the most taxing chore of the week for the wives and maids of England. Washday begins with heating the water. Some of the houses in which I worked in my past positions had a small room called a scullery at the back of the kitchen where an enormous metal tub called a 'copper' was brought to boiling on a gas burner. In houses without a scullery, the water was heated on the kitchen stove. One of my houses had no connection to piped municipal water. There I hauled water into the house from an outside pump for each stage of the laundry process.

Before I added the load of laundry, I chipped soap into the tub of boiling water. I then removed stains by pounding the fabric with a washing dolly that resembled a milking stool on a stick. Once the stains were gone, I ran the soaked clothing through a mangle, a combination of two rollers running in opposite directions, to remove as much water as possible. I then discarded the water from the washtub and added newly boiled water for the rinsing. I washed the light clothing first so that I could use the rinse water for the next load of clothing. After the load was rinsed, I once again ran it through the mangle.

The clean wet laundry was then hung to dry, ideally on the lines strung in the back garden but, whenever rain was pouring down or threatened, on lines strung high in the kitchen. When the laundry was nearly dry, I removed the clothes' pegs and rolled the clothing and linens to prepare for the next day's chore—ironing.

Your American washing machines sound wonderful.

I wonder if women in your country need maids at all with such modern electrical helpers.

I was very surprised but not offended by your question about the relationship between the Malthorpes. However, your comments did give me pause. I will try to describe their relationship. I would not say that Mr. Malthorpe is a 'cruel miscreant' but their relationship can certainly not be described as loving. They treat each other more like business acquaintances than marriage partners. I sense no acrimony between them and I would certainly be privy to any yelling or loud arguments since sounds carry very well in this house.

Harriet and George Malthorpe are as different as chalk and cheese. Harriet is tall and slender and seems unattached to the things and the people around her. George, swarthy and a stone or two overweight, is an outgoing, friendly man who stops to talk with everyone he passes on the street. She stands straight as a ramrod; he slouches. Her hygiene is impeccable; his questionable. She is a person of impulse; he is a slave to routine. Their marriage appears to be one of convenience. I have never seen passion between them. In fact, they interact very little.

The homes of my former employers easily gave up their family secrets. Pictures, notes left strewn about, diaries open to their daily entries all openly revealed the lives of my previous families. What the houses didn't explain was filled in by visitors, offhand comments, and certainly by the children who told all as they gathered around me in the kitchen. Some of the women I worked for talked freely to me about their lives and I enjoyed that very much.

Here I keep myself to myself, not wanting to give away how undemanding my position really is. Last week I was approved for a postal box. From now on you may write to me at: Postal Box 37, Brackham Wood.

I send my love and ask you to please pass it along to my treasured American family.

Moira

*****

October 31, 1937

My Dear Moira,

I'm glad you have a permanent postal box. It was lovely of the Postmistress to hold your mail. This way you are more secure and have much more privacy.

I'm still laughing about "geyser," pronounced "geezer" in Britain. In this country, a "geezer" is a derogatory word for an old man! It's amusing that we both speak "English," but our words often have very different meanings.

The boys have been back in school for almost a month. Willy is in Grade Three this year, while Bert has just entered First Grade. They attend a wonderful school, which just seven years ago, added four more classrooms and an auditorium. Bert was somewhat reluctant to remain all day, but when he learned that his brother would be there as well, he dried his tears and with much bravado, marched into the classroom. Bert is always happier when he is doing exactly what his older brother is. Their school, Hutton, is very unusual in that it's of Spanish design, complete with tiled roof, an arched entry porch and stucco facade. It has only two floors; unlike the other schools in the area, which have at least three, are made of brick and resemble factory buildings.

Living on the West Coast, I have been less exposed to professional discrimination. Although not all physicians in our town have accepted women into the practice of medicine, female physicians are not an unknown in Spokane, merely a rarity.

The first female physician in Spokane was Dr. Mary Latham who began practicing in Spokane in 1887. Another female physician is Dr. Elizabeth White who returned to Spokane just a few years ago to open an office.

With the boys at school during the day, I have much more freedom. I do have a woman in to care for Catherine on the days I'm in the Clinic. On the days I'm at home, Catherine is content to play where I can watch her. It would be lovely to have childcare for her every day, so I'm still considering hiring Sarah, the patient of whom I spoke.

I have learned more about Sarah. It is not a gentle story. Her family left Germany where they had lived in Bergenhaus. I don't know how they all managed to leave, what with the cost of passage for five, but Sarah told me that her father owned a very large company, which manufactured crackers of some sort.

She also told me that once Adolph Hitler became Chancellor of Germany in 1933, German Jews were forbidden to earn a living, among other things. I am guessing that the family must be Jewish, otherwise why would they leave a profitable business? The situation is very alarming, but one would think that someone in Germany would be able to stop the madness of what seems to be happening. How does

Hitler have such control over the German people? It's horrifying!

The case of the Malthorpes becomes stranger. Does Harriet go out shopping during the day? Does she play Bridge, meet friends for tea or just an hour of conversation?

The village in which you live sounds quite small, so I can't imagine where she could find much in the way of clothing. In Spokane, there is a lovely department store called The Crescent. It carries the latest fashions and clothing for the entire family: shoes, fabrics, books, kitchenware, and much more. From your description of Harriet, it doesn't seem likely that she would settle for anything less than the latest styles.

As for Mr. Malthorpe, what is his occupation? He sounds like a rather interesting character, compared to his wife.

Moira, you must follow them some day! One at a time of course! How wonderfully exciting that would be! It would be just like the day, so long ago, that we followed your neighbor, Mr. Greenaway. Do you remember? Mr. Malthorpe probably goes somewhere more exciting than to the Bank each day at 2:00, as Mr. Greenaway did.

My love,
Margaret

*****

November 15, 1937

Dearest Margaret,

I trust that both Willy and Bert are doing well in school this year. I am sure that both boys and Catherine are bright and clever.

I am very happy that Sarah and her family were able to flee Europe at the time that they did. From what I hear, little by little, the Jews are being stripped of their power and freedoms. I wonder if her preoccupation could be caused by worries over what is happening to her family and friends left behind. I fear those worries would be well founded.

I have recently been kept busy with preparations for the upcoming holidays: making paper chains with which to decorate the tree on Christmas Eve, baking mince pies and assembling ingredients for the plum pudding. I doubt if the Malthorpes would celebrate Christmas and Boxing Day if they were left on their own. However, each year Harriet's brother Malcolm visits from London to celebrate and they participate in all the regular rituals. It was at Christmas last year that I heard one personal fact about the family. Malcolm and George knew each other because they both worked for the Inland Revenue and it was through Malcolm that George and Harriet met. Malcolm's visits bring a welcome change from the routine the rest of the year.

In your last letter, you suggested that I try to follow Harriet Malthorpe as you and I once did Mr. Greenaway. It awakened a wonderful memory of hiding behind hedges and crossing back and forth over the lane, thinking he could not see us.

Perhaps it is my timid nature, but I could not discern a way to follow Harriet. One sunny day I plucked up my courage and asked Maggie, who works for the Rutledge family, if I could borrow her bicycle to explore the roads on the outskirts of town. I determined that the shallow terrain would make it impossible to follow Mrs. Malthorpe sight unseen. However, by slightly changing my daily routine on several days, I was able to watch George Malthorpe as he went through his daily activities.

His predictable daily routine begins with a half-mile walk to his haberdashery. He strides briskly but stops to talk to townsfolk on his way. He unlocks his shop at 9:00 sharp, remains within until 1:00 when he leaves for lunch after hanging a closed sign on the doorknob. He returns from lunch promptly at 2:00, and resumes working until he locks the doors at 6:00, finishes his closing paperwork and leaves for home at 6:30, arriving at 7:00.

Harriet, on the other hand, never follows the same routine for two days in a row. There are days when she shops, days when she stays in and reads and writes, days when she takes her bicycle and rides out of the village for exercise. Very rarely she invites one or two ladies over for morning coffee. She completely ignores teatime.

I can allow that she varies her routine but cannot fathom her detachment from four o'clock tea. Never have any of my former employers or, for that matter, anyone I know, failed to take their daily tea break. Even Mrs. Breckinridge, an 80-year-old woman who lives alone at the top of the street, prepares herself a proper tea every day.

Did your parents continue to take tea every afternoon once they came to America? Do you keep up the tradition? I find it a most comforting ritual, taking me back to my childhood.

I must close this letter as I am about to go to the shop where I keep my postal box.

I wish you and your loved ones a very Happy Christmas and look forward to hearing from you once again.

Much love,
Moira

*****

December 15, 1937

Dear Moira,

I am crossing my fingers for luck so that this letter and a package I am also mailing will reach you in time for Christmas. We all wish you the very loveliest of holidays and hope that the New Year brings you good health and much happiness.

The boys are going to be angels in their school's Christmas Pageant. Charles and I both giggled over the casting. Angels? Not our boys! The last month has kept them very busy with school and their Boy Scout Troop activities. Both of their Troops have been gathering food and clothing for the needy. We are very proud of their efforts and are grateful to their Scoutmaster for his leadership.

Sarah seems to be slowly coming out of her shell. Though she has not yet found employment, she has begun to volunteer in our Clinic. Her time engaged in conversation with others in the Clinic has given her more confidence and has certainly made it easier for her to communicate her thoughts. We find her very useful as a translator for other German patients.

I agree that perhaps she is very concerned about family left behind. She has mentioned that her father has two brothers and her mother, a sister.

The mother's sister has immigrated to South Africa of all places. For several weeks I didn't inquire about the extended family, but as we have become better acquainted I have learned that the aunt is married to a diamond broker, hence the move to South Africa. I fear that Sarah's father's brothers are those who are in danger. The world seems to be on the edge of something untoward!

My goodness! You are to be congratulated on your sleuthing. Where does George lunch? With whom does he lunch? Do you know any of the wait staff in his eating establishment? Perhaps they have overheard something that would explain the curious Malthorpes?

Perhaps this Malcolm fellow could be encouraged to lend some hints of his sister and brother-in-law's odd habits? With just the tiniest clue about Harriet's day, you may have much more insight into their unusual behavior. Have you thought of following her in disguise? You could always fool me with funny hats you found in the attic. Sometimes I mistook you for a boy!! I'm certain that you could still tuck your hair into a hat.

Mrs. Malthorpe is too unpredictable in her behavior, if you ask me. She must be hiding something! Do be careful!

We no longer stop for tea. I suppose you will find it shocking, but at 4:00 we are still hard at work. At that hour, the children are at play or some after-school activity. We rarely gather as a family until at least five. This does not mean that we have forgotten teatime altogether. Often ladies' groups will gather for "a tea." However, teas in this country are usually to benefit some cause or to create a very special afternoon for one's friends. Even my mother gave up the ritual. I suppose it was because she and Papa wanted to be like all of our American neighbors!

We are taking the children north to a little town called Newport to chop an evergreen tree for our living room; then we will have the fun of decorating it! We have strung plenty of popcorn and cranberries, and the children, like you, have made paper chains. We gathered pinecones from our yard in late October and tied ribbon on them so they too could be placed on the tree. Even little Catherine helped with that task! I have made over fifteen pomanders from oranges and cloves. The room will smell wonderfully festive with pine and clove.

Again, my darling Moira, we send our love and best wishes for the merriest Christmas.

With love,
Margaret

*****

December 29, 1937

Dearest Margaret,

Your boys no doubt made wonderful angels and I can visualize you, Charles and Catherine beaming with pride as you watched them in the Christmas pageant. It must have been inspiring to see your beautiful tree reflected in the bright eyes of your three excited children.

The great distance between you and your parents must prevent you from spending holidays together. Curiosity led me to the library to study the map of the United States on which I found both Chicago and Spokane. I was astounded to discover that you were separated from your childhood home by the unfathomable distance of 2,000 miles. Heavens! If I travelled that far, I would find myself in an entirely different world several hundred miles east of Moscow, Russia, after having traveled through the borders of France, Germany and Poland. I have not been 50 miles from the town where I was born. My images of London come from books, pictures and the descriptions I hear on the wireless.

This year's Christmas celebration was the most enjoyable I have spent with this childless family. Perhaps it was because your letters have opened my eyes to new possibilities. At Harriet's brother Malcolm's insistence, I participated in all family events including in the after-church tree lighting ceremony. That afternoon, after cooking the dinner of roast goose, Brussels sprouts, roast potatoes, parsnips, and bread sauce, I was asked to join the family. For the first time in many years, I sat at a family Christmas table, rather than eating alone in the kitchen. I must admit that I enjoyed it very much.

Even though the holidays put a temporary halt on my sleuthing, I learned a bit more about my employers. On Boxing Day, George, Malcolm, and Harriet talked freely as we ate the leftovers of the previous day's feast. Even though Malcolm has been here for the past two Christmases, I learned nothing about him until this year. He and Harriet had seemed like strangers to one another. Now I discover that, in fact, they were strangers. Though he doesn't look it, Malcolm is ten years older than Harriet. Did you know that upper class English families send their sons away to school at the age of eight, allowing them to return home only at holidays? Since Harriet was not born until two years after Malcolm left home, they were both raised as only children.

For a short time after completing her schooling, Harriet had been sent to Switzerland to be 'finished.' European finishing schools prepare upper and middle class girls for the lives they are to live, offering training in etiquette, drawing, music, polite conversation, and dance among other things. When she returned, she and Malcolm did not recognize each other. Since their parents died while Harriet was in Switzerland, they had virtually nothing in common save a few shared memories and their Aunt Jewell in Twickenham. I sat in shock and disbelief as I heard about Harriet's education since she displays none of the social graces that she should have been taught.

George talked of his own happy childhood here in Brackham Wood before he, too, was sent away to public school. Being bundled off to Hurstpierpoint at the age of eight was a great shock to him as it had been for generations of English boys. And, like the others, he eventually became accustomed to it: never really happy but seldom miserable.

As the only child in his family he inherited this house and his father's haberdashery when his mother passed away. It was then that he came here and married Harriet.

Harriet revealed nothing of herself during the conversation so I left the table with more questions than I brought to it, particularly about her social graces and deportment.

I send you many good wishes for 1938. May this year bring peace and the dissipation of the storm that seems to be gathering on the other side of the Channel.

With love,
Your Cousin Moira

*****

February 2, 1938

My Dear Moira,

We do have to travel great distances to cross our country; at its widest point it is thirty-four hundred miles wide! It is especially difficult to have Father and Mummy so far away in Chicago, but Father, somehow, always manages to secure a speaking engagement during the Christmas hiatus and then he and Mummy join us for the holiday.

This year they were in Minneapolis for a meeting, before catching the Empire Builder, a Great Northern Railroad Line train, to Spokane. Besides my work at the Clinic, I am also a Great Northern Surgeon. I am not a surgeon; rather, I have been hired by the railroad company to care for their employees. I am paid a small monthly stipend, but I also have a benefit that allows me to travel by train at no cost; and when accompanying me, my family travels at no cost as well. During summer when the children are not in school, we can travel by train to Chicago to visit Mummy and Father.

Today Spokane looks like a frosted fairyland with several inches of snow on the roadways. It's been this way for over a month! The scenery is wonderful; however, it makes it difficult to get around.

Your Christmas meal sounded delicious. I might have a difficult time getting my family interested in roast goose and parsnips, but I have always exposed the children to a variety of dishes, lest they become finicky eaters.

Do you remember Wills Barrow? I think that the Barrows lived perhaps five or six doors from your home? I recall his mother mashing his peas, carrots, and potatoes together so that he would eat them. He was at least four years older than we, and at twelve, his dear mother was still mashing the concoction for him!

My goodness, Moira, you say you learned a lot about nothing at your Christmas dinner table. I think you may have learned something and do not yet know how it fits in with your employer's curious behavior.

Harriet is going somewhere and doing something; neither of which you have yet to discover. Her behavior and demeanor do not fit with her supposed "finishing school" education. Perhaps it was not she who came back from Switzerland! What would have prevented the Harriet you know, from taking the place of the real Harriet? Considering the age difference between Malcolm and his sister and the fact that adolescents change quickly, no wonder he did not recognize her! Maybe she is not really his sister! Or, perhaps neither is who they say they are?!

Are you allowed vacation days? I hope so! You must find a reason to go to London. It will take courage to travel outside your world of Brackham Wood but if you do, then you can see for yourself whether Malcolm lives where he told you he lives. Perhaps you could even, with some diligent sleuthing, discover information about Harriet and Malcolm's parentage!

Onward, my dear, Cousin! An adventure awaits you, not to mention a trip to London!

With love,
Margaret

*****

March 17, 1938

My Dear Margaret,

Pardon me for not writing for such a long time. Our weather has been uncomfortable. A biting wind has been blowing in for more days than I can count, making my daily walk to the shops much longer and less pleasant. I do return home more quickly, with the wind beating at my back but the daily work takes more out of me. I will welcome the coming of spring more than usual this year.

I am much relieved to hear that, despite the considerable distance between you and your parents, your position with the railroad and Uncle Basil's speaking schedule allow you to be together often. I am sure that he and Aunt Elizabeth are thrilled to be able to see you and their beautiful grandchildren more than once a year.

I realize how staid and regular my life has become. I wonder if it would be more like yours had my parents lived and had we had joined you and your family in Chicago. No use to waste time thinking of what is not. "If wishes were horses, beggars would ride."

How interesting that you mentioned Wills Barrow. He lives here yet and I am quite certain that he has learned to eat his vegetables whole. His parents have both passed away and he now works with animals at the larger houses in the area. He has become something of a specialist who is called in to help lame horses recover. I occasionally see him in the village and we often greet each other on the street.

Your statements about Harriet awaken my mind to new questions. I did somewhat wonder if she had changed identity as Malcolm described meeting her again after she had been away to Switzerland.

He also mentioned that their family pictures were destroyed when the barn in which they had been stored burned. I have seen no personal items in this house. How different from other homes where I have been. All of the other women for whom I have worked, even those who lived in mean little houses, kept a few small objects: a plate or brooch from their mother, their father's cuff links, school mementos, or some other bibelot from their past.

But then again, there are certain people who are by nature not warm and loving, who do not identify with objects, and who would rather be off on their own. Perhaps I am one of them; making few friends and feeling very little regret when leaving a family, even after working for them for several years.

In some ways the Malthorpe's weekday routine seems to mimic those of others living in the town. Harriet comes to breakfast each morning dressed for the day and eats at the same table as George, though few words pass between them. He then sits and reads the paper he had picked up earlier from the corner newsstand, sometimes marking an article for Harriet by turning down a corner of the page. So hungry am I for information about my employers that I have searched the paper pile later to peruse the marked pages. I am becoming desperate to find something, anything that would give me a clue to what is going on.

I do spend much of my thinking time hypothesizing how Mrs. Malthorpe spends her bicycling afternoons. If she were a more sociable type, I would guess that she was meeting a friend, maybe even a lover on those long afternoons. If she appeared to be a competitive type, I would have thought that she was trying to beat her best time on a ten-mile loop. Yet she appears to be neither. I must keep trying.

I have never taken a holiday but perhaps it would be possible. Each year George and Harriet leave for a fortnight, which they spend in a seaside resort. The only other time they leave town is on the 20th of the month when they take a day trip to visit Aunt Jewell in Twickenham. They never discuss these visits after they return, which is a frustration for me. In my other households, spirited debate followed every visit to relatives.

I trust that you are enjoying the waning of winter and the anticipation of spring. Please express my greetings to all in your family.

Lovingly
Your cousin,
Moira

*****

April 20, 1938

My Dear Moira,

Spring has finally arrived in Spokane and the city is readying itself for its first Lilac Festival. Our local Garden Club is sponsoring a flower show and a parade through the downtown streets. They are calling it the "Lilac Festival." Lilac trees grow in abundance here, the first lilac being brought to the city in 1906 by J.J. Browne, an early settler. In the spring, our neighborhood, as well as others across the city, is colored with shades of purple, lilac, and the occasional white varietal. The scent is heavenly! The children are so excited about the parade that

they can hardly contain themselves. The event will be held in May, at the peak of the lilacs' color.

Charles' Regiment (the Washington National Guard) has been notified that the annual field training exercises held at Camp Murray, near Seattle, will be extended from the annually scheduled two weeks to four weeks!

This is alarming news as there was no explanation for the extension given. These men are citizen-soldiers whose activities in the past have been limited to monthly drills. About four years ago, they were involved with strike duty in Tacoma, a city also near Seattle, as a result of the lumber industry's labor disputes. For Charles to spend four weeks away from the office is unheard of. The fact that he is away from his desk places his responsibility on others. He says little but I know that he is concerned.

Sarah has experienced another tragedy in her young life; her father, after many months of waiting, finally received word from family in Germany. The information was heartbreaking. One of his two brothers has been missing for three months. He just vanished into thin air, leaving a wife and three young children. Our papers report that over 250,000 Jews have already fled from Germany and Austria and that thousands more are attempting to leave. Sarah's family does not think that the brother would have fled the country without his family. They are assuming the worst has happened.

I have stayed busy with Clinic work, managing the house, my gardening, and of course the children. My life is quite boring, however, compared to what is going on in your life. You now have the perfect excuse to discover the solution to the questions you have about the mysterious Malthorpes. By taking some time away from your position, when they take time to go to the beach, you may well discover the true identity of Harriet. From all that you have told me, I think that Harriet is the key. Two weeks will be ample time to investigate the "Aunt Jewell" connection to George and Harriet. Why do they visit her the 20th of every month? Does she really exist?

A simple excursion to Twickenham in one of Wills' wagons for a few hours, would give you plenty of time to "snoop"; not to mention a pleasant outing with Wills! Really Moira, you must find a way to meet more of your neighbors if you want to have any hope of getting answers to your questions. You have time on your hands, your responsibilities are limited, and no one questions your time away from your station.

By the way, do you know where the Blake family home was located? What about a trip there? Churchyards and church registers reveal much. Can you confirm the existence of the "finishing school" Harriet and Malcolm "say" she attended? The Library should give you that information. A trip to London or even to Switzerland might suit you!!!

With love and great excitement about your investigative adventures,

Cousin Margaret

*****

May 30, 1938

My Dearest Margaret,
How good to hear from you.

Inspired by your encouragement, I had been considering beginning an herbaceous border in the front garden. Neither of the Malthorpes offered any objections and it would make a nice addition to the neighborhood. It would also allow me to comfortably integrate further into Brackham Wood. Puttering in the garden, asking for advice, and admiring the plantings of the neighbors will provide me a natural way to be out and about and to begin integrating into the community.

After much thought, I have decided instead to create a cottage garden because a formal herbaceous border, while beautiful, consumes a tremendous amount of labour. A cottage garden, however, is planted with self-seeding annuals, which can be interspersed with vegetables. I feel ready for the challenge, even though I have not lifted a spade since my parents passed away nearly twenty years ago. As I secretly plan my trip to London, I will include the dream of every gardener: a visit to Kew Gardens.

Another stop I plan to make will be at Somerset House, the repository for all birth, marriage, and death certificates since 1837. I am becoming excited to step into the place.

How you will miss Charles while he is away for four weeks training. I imagine that his reporter's mind will be at work as he undergoes an additional two weeks of soldiering this summer. I am concerned about the slowly increasing emphasis on military activity in our two countries but I also fear it may be necessary. As you no doubt have learned, German soldiers have marched into and overtaken Austria without a shot being fired.

The 'anschluss,' announced by Hitler on March 12, has been terrible for the Jewish population of Austria, especially in Vienna. Word is reaching here of terrible humiliations, and even deaths perpetrated by the brown clad German soldiers. I pray that the members of Sarah's family have not been treated so poorly but I must report that the situation is very, very bad.

I am happy to report that, prodded by your comments, I am becoming more outgoing, in my own quiet way. I now take longer with my shopping and walk with my head up, rather than looking down and charging ahead. As I meet people's eye and nod, they sometimes stop to chat; it is as if I am a brand newcomer to the village.

One day, Wills Barrow stopped to visit for a few minutes. I learned from him, and later others, that he had been married but that his wife and child both died tragically during childbirth about 15 years ago. He is a serious and stable man who has managed to stay afloat by helping with lame horses and moving goods from place to place using two Daimler lorries built during the Great War. Keeping them both in good repair must be the most difficult part of his business.

Please give my love to all of my American relatives.

With love,

Moira

*****

July 1, 1938

Dear Cousin Moira,

I'm so sorry that it has taken so long for me to answer your letter. The Lilac Festival time kept me very busy along with the beginning of summer vacation for the children, and other activities, which I shall endeavor to describe herein. I am hoping that this letter does not take as long to reach you, as your

last letter took to reach me! Your cottage garden may already have brought forth blooms by the time you read this!

What a grand idea the garden is! And what a good way to gather information from neighbors and townsmen about your employers! I do hope you have some details in your next letter! I would think that any information or names of people unknown to you, but learned through your conversations, should be taken to Somerset House and researched; and of course you will start with surnames of your employer and his wife, won't you?

Charles returned from Reserve Duty with all sorts of gossip, most of which, if it is true, is extremely frightening. The prospect of war is almost unbelievable, but the world events of late indicate that it is all too true and that we really are on a path of horrid consequences. Of course, most here feel that the U.S. will never be involved, but I fear for you, my dear cousin! We were so happy to have him home that for a brief time we forgot about what he had heard.

Recently several children have come to our Clinic manifesting various forms of orthopedic problems. We are not as well-prepared to care for them as the mobile unit of the Shriners, an arm of Freemasonry in the United States.

Not having their own structure, the Shriners have rented beds for the young patients in a local hospital. We are able to refer the children we've seen to the mobile unit for care. Most of their conditions are polio resultant; however some are related to infected bones or tuberculosis of the joint.

The Shriners have been fundraising for years by collecting tin foil and sending it to Chicago to be melted into tin alloy bars. The last shipment was over 10,000 pounds! They now have raised enough funds to build their own hospital, which will care for more than just the 20 children who have been lucky enough to find space in the rented beds of St. Luke's Hospital. The permanent Shriners Hospital is expected to open some time next year.

Sarah has taken a keen interest in these unfortunate children. I referred her for a job, with pay, in the mobile unit. She was hired and I'm told she has found a niche. Eventually, I'm certain that she will move to the new hospital. Her depression has all but disappeared, now that she has found that there are children less fortunate than she. Amazing!

Moira, now that you have found a way to secure more information in your village, I believe it important for you to learn to drive an automobile. Who better than Wills to teach you? He has a lorry, no, two lorries, and certainly you have the time to be available for lessons anytime he is not making deliveries. Better yet, why not accompany him on his route occasionally and learn while he's at work. With the way the world is shaping itself, it is extremely important that you be prepared in every way that you can!

Are you attracted to him in the least? I suppose it could be problematic were he to be attracted to you and you not to him. If the latter is the case, you must make your intentions very clear. *You only want to learn to drive.*

With love,
Margaret

*****

September 30, 1938

Dear Margaret,

How happy I was to receive your letter and to learn that Sarah is getting her feet on the ground. Helping others is certainly the best way to help oneself. Cases of the 'infantile paralysis,' which is also called polio, have been growing here in England as well.

Here in England our village greens are places of activity. They vary greatly in size and description. The smallest consist of only a small patch of lawn on which grows a tree, with a simple bench beneath. The largest hold cricket fields, open spaces for village fetes, play areas for children and allotments where those who live in flats can plant and tend to vegetable gardens.

The green here in Brackham Wood is a bit of all of these things. However, last week it began to change. Unsightly excavations began to appear at the end of the green near the school. Jeb Hastings, foreman of the crew doing the digging, has not the slightest idea of the purpose of this project that is causing much discussion among us as we go about our daily shopping.

I wonder if this drastic change in this very predictable village life has anything to do with those events on the Continent that are leaving me so very unsettled. Our Prime Minister Neville Chamberlain, while he speaks of peace with Germany and insists that we should not fear Adolph Hitler, is behaving as if quite the opposite is true.

Yesterday Chamberlain met with Hitler, Mussolini and the French Premier, Eduoard Daladier. In an attempt to pacify Hitler, he signed the Munich Pact thus allowing Germany to annex the Sudetenland, the area of Czechoslovakia bordering on Germany where many German-speaking people have lived for centuries. No representative of Czechoslovakia was invited to this meeting.

Many of my fellow villagers listen to Chamberlain's words and believe that Hitler can be appeased while I, by watching his actions, come to a very different conclusion. First Austria and now the Sudetenland. I see signs all round me that we are on the way to another war with Germany.

Many prominent English citizens, particularly those of the upper classes, have become enamored of Hitler. His well-organized public spectacles and Germany's efficiency of manufacturing and transportation impress them greatly. They truly believe that he and Mussolini have made the trains run on time, even though this is far from proven fact.

My life has changed drastically since my last letter. I did indeed begin on the cottage garden with the result that I have suddenly begun to see the townspeople in quite another way. The minute I stepped out and began working in the front garden, neighbors and passers by began to stop and inquire as to what I was doing and, when they heard of my goal and my lack of knowledge, they literally flooded me with advice and some have even been so generous as to bring me cuttings from their own gardens.

We now have a respectable looking patch with the tall plants at the back and shorter more colorful varieties at the front. Now, rather than spending hours sitting indoors and reading, I am outside planning, planting, weeding, cutting and tending my new project. Wills has stopped by several times to check on my progress and we have established an easy conversation between the two of us.

I think that you will be surprised at what you read next. Your letters have always encouraged me to be braver, to try more things, to become an actor upon the worlds' stage rather than just an observer. Little by little I have begun such transitions. But, my dear cousin, you will be amazed to learn that I took one of your suggestions even before I had read it.

One day as Wills and I were talking in the front garden, he suggested that we take a ride in the one of his two lorries that was in good repair. The following Sunday we took a short ride to the neighboring village of Steyning where he asked if I had ever driven a motorized vehicle. When I confessed that I had scarcely even ridden in one, he insisted that I move to the driver's seat. He then began to identify the different parts of the lorry. We have done the same activity three times and now I can, by pushing on the clutch pedal and pressing on the gas pedal ever so slightly, make that gigantic vehicle move a few feet. I feel my confidence build as Wills encourages, but does not force. Each week after I return home, I write down what I have learned and for the rest of the week I practice pushing imaginary pedals and shifting imaginary gears.

So I can report to you that I am beginning to make a bit of progress toward driving: a very unusual activity for the fair sex of Brackham Wood. Women do not generally operate such machinery although Mrs. Minstock does drive the farm tractor and has been known to bring it to town pulling a wagonload of produce to sell when there is an abundant crop.

Struggling to control that giant lorry has made me aware that I need to become more physically fit. Before I came to Malthorpe's house, the tremendous physical work required to haul water and to do laundry for large families kept me in top shape. These last three years of sitting and reading have done nothing to maintain my strength.

I am anxiously waiting for the Malthorpes to schedule their annual holiday at the seaside. I would have expected them to have already taken it if previous years were any indication. However, they have both been home less often in the past few weeks.

I do appreciate your warning me not to let any false impression arise about the feelings between Wills and me. As you know, I am very inexperienced in these matters but I am quite certain that he looks upon me as I do him—as the sibling that neither of us had. While I think there is nothing to be concerned about, I will heed your advice as you have much more experience in this area than I.

I am becoming more interested in the people and things around me just as the world seems to be disintegrating. I save money for my future dream but have begun to grapple with the present. I feel happier and more energetic even as trenches appear in the village green and as Germany continues to add square miles to her borders.

May I be so bold as to quote Charles Dickens as he begins 'A Tale of Two Cities:' "It was the best of times; it was the worst of times."

So, dearest Margaret, you can see the delicious predicament in which I now find myself. Please give my love to Charles, the children and to your parents.

Much love and many good wishes,
Your Cousin Moira

*****

October 16, 1938

My Dearest Moira,

I am so proud of you! I know how much strength it took for you to break away from your zone of comfort, not to mention breaking with convention. You are a very courageous woman. I guarantee that all this effort will put you in good stead and someday perhaps will be skills that will save your life, or that of someone else.

For example, the boys took swimming lessons this summer at the pool in nearby Comstock Park. While waiting for them to complete their lessons, I watched older students taking Red Cross lessons in the deep end of the pool. My thought at that time was that our children will follow the same path of learning because some day they may need those skills to save a swimmer in trouble. You do not need to be young to learn a new skill.

Your Mr. Chamberlain's actions have been *the* topic of conversation everywhere in our country. His name has been front page news for weeks. Now his "piece of paper" is nothing more than a "scrap of paper." I agree with you, war is inevitable. I fear for you, dear Moira!

The curious activities of your employers, or lack thereof, and their more frequent disappearances of late are very disconcerting to me, as I know they are to you. Do you suppose there is any possibility that they are agents embedded by the Germans to "watch and wait"? In light of Hitler's most recent actions in Czechoslovakia and Austria, I wouldn't doubt that such a plan had been put in place in many villages and cities in England, and elsewhere for that matter. I wonder whether you yourself could serve some purpose to your government should war actually be declared. You certainly have an established "cover," so to speak. Who would ever suspect *you* of being an agent?

I am very curious to learn the purpose of the trenches being dug in your village. I can't imagine for what they will be used and why all the secrecy.

The alarming events developing in Europe have spilt over into Spokane. Our newspaper describes the protesters here as wearing Nazi-style grey shirts. Most likely, they are fascist Silver Shirts who were seen marching on our main downtown street. Because of Hitler's actions, prominent members of our Jewish community have already brought more than 50 German Jews to Spokane. That is laudable, but what isn't laudable is that some Jews here have even been blocked from membership in some social clubs. What's more, restrictive covenants prevent them from buying homes in some areas.

On the positive side, however, we do have a well-known Jewish dentist, David Cowen, who is serving in our state legislature. He was first elected in 1935. I hear that he will most likely be re-elected.

Racial intolerance has affected the Japanese population as well. In fact, our power company recently felt it necessary to "assure its customers that it employed no Japanese workers!" There are only 300+ Japanese families remaining in Spokane today.

On a more uplifting note, the children are doing well. They are happy and glad to be back in school with their friends. Catherine will be ready to begin school next fall! It is truly amazing how quickly the time has flown.

I know you have been squirreling away portions of your wages to use for your London adventure when and if your employers ever go to the beach.

But once you've used those funds, you will have to start saving all over again. This will help to do just that.

Moira, please accept the wire of funds that I will send. I'm certain that your postmistress can accept the wire. It is not much, but it will provide funds to start an additional account. Charles and I recommend that you have two accounts in the event that your activities are ever questioned by the Malthorpes.

Perhaps by wiring gifts to you, they will not take as long as letters do, nor will they have the chance to disappear altogether! I assume you have just one bank in Brackham Wood. Is there a village nearby which has a bank that you can use for the second account? Please send wiring instructions from whichever bank you chose to use.

With love,
Margaret

*****

November 16, 1938

My Dearest Margaret,

There is much to tell you in this letter, but first I must address your most generous offer. Six months ago I would definitely have thanked you kindly but declined. However, recent events have caused me to accept with the assurance that I will most certainly repay the debt in the future. With all the changes in the world and the uncertainty ahead, I feel it would be foolish to let my pride keep me from accepting this gift. The Steyning Post Office is the best place to wire the money. It is a pretty little village just across the river, not two miles from here. I shall open a postal savings account there once the money arrives.

Wills and I seem to have made a habit of meeting on Sunday afternoons. We began this week with a drive to Shoreham Airport. We drank tea in the lovely cafeteria while gazing at the Lancing College Chapel, sometimes called the Cathedral of the Downs. Wills now seems to be spending less time working with lame horses and more time moving goods with his lorries.

We still do not know the purpose of the excavations in the village green. They have now been fenced off to keep townsfolk from falling in. The holes have been there for so long that no one remarks upon them any more.

Though my cottage garden has been put to bed in preparation for the winter, the connections it helped me forge with others in the village continue.

My employers seem to be back to their usual behavior after months of being away more than usual. Harriet is now gone every afternoon like clockwork and, rain or shine, does not return until dinner is on the table. Your hypotheses about my employers have caused me much reflection. I have come up with even more questions. Is their strange marriage real? Are they working for a government and, if so, is it for our own defense or are they working for the Germans? Again, I ask myself why their home gives no clues.

I am distressed to read that discrimination against those of Jewish background is obvious even in the far western part of the United States. Both of our countries have failed to act positively to help the situation.

The Jewish people of Austria and Germany were encouraged when they learned that Franklin Roosevelt had initiated a conference in Evian in July where representatives from 32 countries met to discuss the growing numbers of Jewish refugees fleeing the Nazis. Upon hearing of the conference, Hitler said that if other countries would take them, he would help them leave. Neither of our countries agreed to take in substantial numbers of these refugees.

As far as I can discern, our Christmas holidays will be spent the same way as last. Malcolm's visit will no doubt brighten things up. This year has passed with no mention of my employer's annual holiday trip to the seaside but I heard them discuss an April journey.

I look forward to hearing about your holidays. Will your children be angels in the Christmas pageant once again?

Much love to all,
Moira

*****

December 10, 1938

Dear Cousin Moira,

I hope you have received the first wire of funds. Please advise whether you were able to accept the transfer without difficulty and I will wire again; this time with a more generous amount. (It could be silly perhaps, to be so paranoid.) At the very least, since the Steyning Post Office is only two miles away, it should be an easy trip for you and one that will not raise red flags...unless of course, someone is reading our mail.

Now that you are able to drive, will it be any easier to follow Harriet on her all-day excursions? Where in heaven's name does she go? It sounds as if you will be waiting until well after the New Year to

do any researching in London of who she and her husband really are! Perhaps the holidays will reveal more insight!

Our Clinic is busier than ever. I am seeing more families of Japanese and Jewish descent than ever before. I suppose it is because they are being refused elsewhere. Though I miss seeing Sarah, I know from others that she is doing well in her position at the Shriners Hospital. She has even been seeing a young man. I have heard nothing more about her family in Germany, although if they have been unable to leave the country, any news might be dreadful.

Charles and I have hired a young Japanese woman named Yoshi Tsutakawa. She is attending Whitworth College and her family lives in Seattle. She will live with us. Although she doesn't cook, she is wonderful with the children. After losing our housekeeper in September and having the responsibility of the house, children, etc. by myself (Charles is helpful, but he doesn't dust!) for several months, Yoshi is a gift! I do worry that her being Japanese could be a problem, but we will not be bullied. She is as much of an American as I am!

Merry Christmas, my dear Moira! All the best in 1939!

With love,
Cousin Margaret

*****

January 20, 1939

My Dearest Margaret,

Thank you so much for your wire to the Steyning Post Office. It came through very quickly and I have opened my postal savings account. I wish you and all of your loved ones a Happy New Year, though I must admit that I have a difficult time accepting that 1939 will be so for England. Many of our villagers seem unaware of the certainty of impending war even though we have all been issued gas masks, men are being called to man anti-aircraft defenses and ships and the rest of us have been asked to contact local authorities to determine in what capacity we can serve. During the Great War the Germans used poison gas and bombed city centers. Our Home Office, no doubt, predicts that they will use the same methods if we go to war with them again.

I certainly hope that our government takes into account the advances in flying. When Neville Chamberlain made three visits to Hitler, his flying time was only three-and-one-half hours between Munich and the Heston Aerodrome. I fear that the English Channel will no longer serve as a treacherous 20 mile-wide moat between here and Europe.

I try to prepare myself for the unavoidable war to come by looking back to the announcements and the publication that the Home Office delivered to us just before Prime Minister Chamberlain signed the Munich Agreement in September. The anti-aircraft, barrage balloon, and coast defense units of the Territorial Army were activated as were the defense units of the Auxiliary Air Force and Observer Corps. All of the officers and men of the RAF were recalled from leave.

Centers were set up where those wishing to sign up would be welcomed. Appeals were sent out for ARP (Air Raid Precaution) wardens, auxiliary firefighters, and ambulance drivers. I looked over the handbook, which gave directions for preparing refuge rooms, fire precautions and suggestions for air raid behavior.

I am pleased to hear that you have some help in the house. Raising three children while working outside the home is more difficult than I can imagine. If I may be so bold I would like to request a photograph of your family so that I can picture them in my mind as I read and think about you all. And should you have a recent image of your parents, it also would be most welcome.

I am thinking of how I could send a photo to you. Perhaps we could see a similarity between ourselves. When we were very young we were sometimes taken for sisters. Perhaps Wills would be able to borrow a camera.

Speaking of Wills, we continue to spend Sunday afternoons together. On the occasional weekend he also attends morning service at St. Peter's Church. Vicar Dimblebey can serve up a good sermon and his singing voice adds spirit to our communally sung hymns. When Wills does come to service, however, he and I act as though we do not recognize each other. I am not sure why we masquerade as strangers. Perhaps we are both afraid that our friendship would be misconstrued as something more. I think we have too much mutual respect to cause embarrassment to one another.

George and Harriet are now here fewer hours even on weekends. During the holidays, however, Malcolm came as usual and we had a wonderful celebration. While I did not learn anything directly from them, I was in and out of the house as usual, always entering and leaving by the kitchen door with the result that I became invisible to them.

On one particular day they were in the sitting room engaged in serious discussion as I slipped into the hallway. They were talking in low voices. The only word I could catch, probably because it was mentioned so often was 'invasion.'

Also, Wills told me of something strange he observed when out on one of his deliveries. While driving through the Downs, he saw Harriet standing on top of a rise practicing arm movements that looked like a dance. He parked his lorry further on down the road, dropped down behind the tall grass and watched as she repeated the same motions over and over.

His observation added more questions for you and me to ponder.

Thank you once again for the money you wired. I could never have believed how good it makes me feel to have relatives who care about me. It gives me a lifting of spirit that I have never before experienced.

May things be well with you.

My love to all,

Moira

*****

March 1, 1939

Dearest Moira,

I'm so glad to learn that the wire went through without a problem of any sort. By now you should have received two other transfers. What does Wills say about your "banking" in Steyning? I wonder whether he raised an eyebrow. You undoubtedly have a good reason to give for walking two miles to bank when you have your own bank in Brackham Wood.

I hope you enjoy seeing the photos of your American cousins and my parents. Do you feel as if I resemble that same cousin of long ago? Has Wills found a camera to borrow? We would love to have a photo of you. Perhaps you could purchase your own

camera. Here in the U.S., one can find a Kodak Brownie camera for about $6.00. What a grand time you could have recording your life in the village!

Charles was in Portland, Oregon, in mid-February to cover a story of the continuing racism toward the Japanese community. It seems to be rearing its ugly head everywhere. Yoshi, my nanny, has expressed fear for her parents who are still in Seattle. They of course, were not born in this country.

Charles' brother, Thomas, is being sent to Vancouver, B.C. to cover the May visit of King George VI and Queen Elizabeth. Some say that their visit is a signal that war is brewing and to remind English-speaking Canadians of their duty to the motherland. What do you make of the visit?

Harriet's actions, recently observed by Wills, have to make one wonder who she is attempting to signal. She is not just dancing on the Downs for the fun of it!! The more you tell me about Harriet, the stranger and perhaps more dangerous she seems to become. Her habits are certainly not those of an ordinary matron living in the countryside of England. You, yourself, could observe something that may seem innocent, but could actually put you in harm's way without ever knowing why. Please take care of yourself; stay warm, and keep a watchful eye on the road when you are walking to Steyning.

With love,
Cousin Margaret

*****

June 1, 1939

Dearest Margaret

Life here has changed dramatically since I last wrote. The hours of leisure that I described last year have almost entirely disappeared, having been taken up by gardening, sewing, and the Women's Volunteer Service.

Fear of war with Germany has reminded me that we are indeed an island nation. The shortages that we suffered from the sinking of supply ships by German submarines during the last war are certain to reoccur. We have a good supply of tinned goods, which I am trying to supplement with every visit to the grocer.

Wills and I are still able to meet on Sundays and now always drive away from Brackham Wood. Some days we even deliver goods to a nearby town on our weekly adventure. You asked if Wills is curious about my walks to Steyning. If he is, he does not comment. I think that is, perhaps, because he is a man.

Two months ago, Mrs. Malthorpe asked me if I could sew. I explained to her that I had sewn for myself as well as some of the children and adults in the households where I had previously been employed. I must admit to you that I had rather liked doing that because while I sewed, another girl was always brought in to perform my maid-of-all-work duties.

Harriet seemed quite pleased. In fact, she is now becoming slightly friendly toward me. I took measurements and ordered enough good cloth for three suits of almost identical design. She also let me choose some fabric with which to sew a warm coat for myself for which I am most grateful as mine is now over ten years old.

She asked me to allow for extra length in the hems, sleeves and all seams as well as making the jacket of each suit one size larger than her measurements. Perhaps she wants to have extra fabric in the wider seams and longer lengths in case upcoming war shortages make fabric very difficult to come by, in which case, she will have me alter the design. I do admit that I enjoy tailoring. I have been called on very little to make such fine clothes. I will also admit to you that my ego is a bit disappointed by her choice of size. No one will praise me for the fine fit of Mrs. M's jackets.

She chose medium grey worsted wool gabardine for one of the suits and Harris tweeds for the other two— the first with blue and red threads running through grey and the second in golden tones. She also asked me to cut the pockets from cotton gabardine, which is quite unusual for a woman's clothing. Typically it is used only in the pockets of men's business suits, which need to be stronger than the flimsy material used in most women's clothing. I am nearly finished with all three suits. I chose to assemble them at the same time, finding that in so doing I can move more quickly.

Over the past three months, I have purchased for myself one new cardigan, two pullovers, and two shirtwaists, so with the coat I will construct with Mrs. Malthorpe's gift of cloth, I shall have a wardrobe that can see me through the next ten years.

Besides gardening and sewing, I have begun helping with the Women's Voluntary Service, in which all women are encouraged to participate. I do not play a large part, only going in on Tuesday afternoons. Just now they are knitting socks and pullovers for the Royal Navy. Not being much of a knitter, I sort incoming yarn for the knitters and make tea to keep them going.

As you read this letter you will understand that I am preparing for war in every way I can imagine; stocking up food without hoarding, working on refreshing my worn out wardrobe, and helping with the WVS every Tuesday. Of course your contributions to my Steyning account have given me additional peace of mind. I have no doubt that war will erupt any minute and am grateful for each additional day of preparation. As you no doubt know, Hitler took over the rest of Czechoslovakia in March and shows no signs of stopping his conquests.

Please accept my gratitude for all of your help and send my love to all.

Moira

P.S. Pardon my scribble but before I was able to post this letter, the Malthorpes announced that they will depart for their holiday on July 1. Once the three suits are completed, they hold no objections to my being gone at the same time. I am hastily sending letters and making preparations for my visit to London. This will be the biggest adventure of my life thus far.

Love,
Moira

*****

August 31, 1939

My Dear Moira,

It's been a long, hot summer and although the children have enjoyed every minute of vacation time, on some nights it's been impossible for anyone, even them, to sleep.

You have again taken to sewing. How lovely! I wish you were here to help me with the children's Halloween costumes. Even as a young girl, you could hand-stitch for your dolls! However, the business of making clothes that don't fit doesn't make sense.

Could Harriet be expecting? If so, why not just increase the waist, but not the sleeves? Why ever would she choose identical styles? Normally, a woman would want something "different" for each of the three suits. The pockets are just as strange. Perhaps she plans to carry stones?!! Oh, Moira, your employer is just a wee bit touched.

By the time you read this, the Malthorpes will have returned from their holiday and you will have returned from yours as well. I am so anxious to hear your news and your description of your adventure in London.

You are juggling many balls at the moment: the garden, the sewing, the housekeeping, the Auxiliary, not to mention the "research" of your employers. Any one of these could lead to putting you in danger. Do be careful.

We hope that this letter finds you well and safe and that we hear from you soon!

With love,
Cousin Margaret

*****

August 31, 1939

Dearest Margaret,

I must write you even though I have not yet received your reply to my last letter.

I have so much to tell you that I scarcely know where to begin. From the moment I posted my last letter to you until today, more has happened than during any other period of my life. On Sunday, July 2, Wills drove me to the Worthing Station. When the London

Train arrived I climbed aboard eagerly and was the first to enter an empty carriage. When I dropped my Gladstone bag onto the padded seat, an enormous dust cloud emerged sending me into a coughing fit and discouraging anyone else from entering. I rode alone until the train reached the next stop at Shoreham at which time a taciturn man and woman joined me. Neither uttered a word for the rest of the journey.

An hour and a half after leaving Worthing, I stepped from the train onto the platform in Victoria Station and felt as though I had entered another world: a feeling that did not leave me until I returned to Brackham Wood one week later and walked through the door of Michelsgrove.

Victoria Station was the largest building I had entered until that moment. Even though I had seen pictures of London I was unprepared for the size and bustle of the city as well as the black coating on all the buildings resulting from millions of coal fires burning on millions of hearths.

I was fortunate to have found lodgings with Mary Anne Withers, the sister of Phoebe Miles, the postmistress of Brackham Wood. For a very reasonable sum I was able to sleep in a nice airy bedroom and eat a delicious breakfast each morning. Therefore, London looked much better to me by the time I left the flat to begin my Monday morning adventures.

When Harriet Malthorpe told her brother Malcolm that I was coming to London, he volunteered to show me the city on Wednesday afternoon. I was able to visit in person places I had seen only in pictures: The Houses of Parliament, Big Ben, St. Paul's Cathedral, Westminster, Piccadilly Circus, Nelson's Column in Trafalgar Square, Tower Bridge, and the Tower of London.

With his excellent directions, I was later also able to visit the British Museum, walk through Kensington Gardens and ride past Buckingham Palace before my visit was over. All of this sightseeing was in addition to my main objective, which was to visit Kew Gardens. Originally when I planned the trip I had intended to learn all that I could about flowers and beautiful gardens. However, with the impending war, I found myself interested in edible plants. The sheer enormity of the gardens was at first overwhelming but I was able to spend many hours there as Mary Anne's home was only a short tube ride away.

At your suggestion, I visited Somerset House and checked on the birth, marriage, and death records of our own family as well as those of George, Malcolm and Harriet. I very much enjoyed finding the dates the same as those in our family Bible. I also found the marriage record for George and Harriet and their birth dates. The parents of Malcolm and Harriet apparently died in the same fire that destroyed their family records.

***

Letter continued—September 25, 1939

***

I was so glad to hear from you. As you may have realized, I wrote the above last month. Before I got it in the post, Germany invaded Poland, and England declared war on Germany.

We assume that the Germans will bomb the large cities and ignore us who are on the flight path. However, there is no certainty. It is entirely possible that we in Britain will also find our lives going up in flames.

I will briefly tell you the changes that have taken place since war was declared on September third and get this letter of reply in the mail as soon as possible.

You and I have established such close rapport during the past two years that I flatter myself in thinking that you may be concerned about my welfare.

We sling the straps of our boxed gas masks over our shoulders whenever we leave home.

I have sewn blackout curtains for every room of the house since no light must shine from our windows lest it serve as a guide to enemy aircraft.

The blackout also means that all automobile headlights must be hooded, which has resulted in many accidents.

All road signs have been removed in the event of a German invasion.

Our large railway station signs have been taken away and replaced by very small signs within each station. They are scarcely visible to the passengers.

Ration books have been issued and we must now trade with only one grocer. This system, which was used in the last war, simplifies food distribution by allowing each grocer only the amount of food to provision his registered customers. However, it is a very difficult adjustment for shoppers like me.

The trenches in the park are now ready for us to jump into in the event of falling bombs.

An air raid shelter has been designated and located very near the schoolyard.

The Women's Voluntary Service (WVS) has stepped up activities, collecting clothing and extra items to be distributed to those who may lose their homes and goods to bombing attacks.

Fifty-seven children have been sent here from inner city London for their own protection. This has been quite a shock to both them and us, which I hope to describe in more detail in a subsequent letter.

Sirens assault us. We frequently practice reacting to the 'take cover' alarm, a continuous tone that rises and falls between a high and a low note, and the 'all clear,' which is a continuous low note.

Our lives here have been turned upside down.

In this time of uncertainty, I want to make certain that you all know how much you all have meant to me: Margaret, Charles, Willy, Bert, Catherine, Elizabeth and Basil.

Love,
Moira

*****

November 20, 1939

My Dearest Moira,

I cannot begin to tell you how very saddened we both are about the horrid situation in our beloved England; in the world for that matter! It must be so upsetting to everyone in your little village, particularly the children. We admire your courage and your perseverance, and can only imagine what our life in Spokane would be like should our country be at war. Thank goodness we do not have to worry about that! When I think about all the changes, regulations and general upheaval in your village, I imagine a very different life compared to that which you have always known.

Our Red Cross Ladies have secured several storage rooms in a downtown warehouse and have begun to knit goods, prepare surgical bandages, and sew hospital gowns; which in turn will be sent overseas. I have several friends

who knit. They always buy their yarn at The Crescent, a downtown department store, which has also jumped in to help by offering yarn at a discount, as well as a room in which to knit.

I do worry about you. But after having written to you for these two years, I know you to be a very capable woman. I am certain that you will survive this, just as you have survived all the other adversity in your life.

I'm so glad that you were able to venture from your home to London before the war began. You saw so much in a very short time, but perhaps that is because you had such an excellent tour guide. Did you see Malcolm only the one Wednesday afternoon? At the very least you can dream of the day that you can return for yet another visit. What did Wills think of your gallivanting off to London?

I suppose I shouldn't bother you with this news, but I too, am grateful for a confidant. So pardon me, please, while I rage.

Yoshi has gone home to Seattle for who knows how long. Fortunately, she has a month before classes begin. Her family is in an upheaval as her older brother, Haruki, has been arrested.

Haruki is a graduate of the University of Washington. During his school years he was quite an activist. I believe it was in 1935, that he was the president of the American Students' Union, which organized protests, meetings, and anti-ROTC campaigns. Their anti-war and anti-fascism gatherings caused so much disruption on campus and in the city of Seattle that the Dean of the School gave their names to the FBI.

Haruki and his confederates had begun the protests again, but this time he was arrested.

There is so much racial intolerance, discrimination, and even violence against the Japanese that I fear for the entire populace; but in particular, for this family. I have yet to hear anything from Yoshi, but then she has only been gone a week. A friend of hers is filling in while she is gone. Sharon is not nearly as efficient as Yoshi and I am certain that should Yoshi's absence go on much longer, I will have to replace Sharon.

I doubt that now that you have travelled alone, learned to drive, and also planted a garden (none of which, I might add, you had ever done), you have much fear of doing anything! But I do hope that you will think a situation through before acting; making certain all your ducks are in a row first!!!

Stay safe my dear cousin.

Love,

Margaret

*****

January 21, 1940

Dearest Margaret,

Thank you for your wonderful letter and your most encouraging words. They lighten my heart each time I read them. The story of Rudolph gives me hope.

We had a curtailed Christmas celebration but Malcolm did visit for a short time, arriving on the morning of Christmas Eve and taking the return train on the evening of Boxing Day. We had little time for the conversations that I so enjoyed during last year's holiday. I had seen him for only a half-day in London last summer but his detailed advice and directions allowed me to make excellent use of time while I was there.

While I hope that you, my loved ones, will never have to experience the terror and privations of war, I harbor the fear that we will soon need your country to step in and help us as you did during the last war. There are those who say that we did not need that help but I remember that my parents and teachers were most grateful for the American help in tipping the balance our way.

I hope to receive news that Yoshi has returned to you. It is frightening to hear that her brother was jailed for speaking his mind in a free country.

Just now our lives have been made very inconvenient by our wartime homeland preparations. While I understand the need for them, some of our neighbors see no reason for it to be that way.

Even though we now live with curtained windows, carry our gas masks upon our persons and are kept from our beaches by wire fences topped with barbed, coiled concertina wire, nothing has happened. For the first ten weeks, I felt as though each night would be my last. However, not one bomb has fallen and some are calling it the "phony war." They talk as if they wish something, anything, would happen; they can't abide the waiting. I myself wonder why Hitler has not yet sent his bombers but am not anxious for him to break the tension by doing so.

My summer trip to London was a great gift. It broadened my horizons. When we were besieged by the 57 cockney children who were evacuated from London for safety, I understood the conditions from which they came and I like to think that I was some help to them and to their hosts here in Brackham Wood.

When they arrived, they were led to the school gymnasium and fed while those villagers who had agreed to take them into their homes gathered on the play yard. I cannot believe that one million children were evacuated from the large cities, particularly London and Liverpool in the first four days following the outbreak of war. Mr. Malthorpe informed me that we were not eligible to take a refugee child; perhaps because we had no spare bedroom. However, he offered no objection to my helping with the feeding and organization of the children who were to arrive.

I wish I had been able to photograph the looks on our neighbor's faces as they caught the first glance of the evacuees. Shock, disgust, and revulsion would not begin to describe their reactions. The children were filthy; their clothing was in tatters, they smelled like stable hands and they spoke an indecipherable language. As the handlers were checking their lists, I had a few words with my neighbors, trying to convince them that the children were washable by describing how easily my clothing had become soiled in the coal dust laden air of London.

Even though bath night is always Saturday night, I believe that exceptions were made and every child was bathed that Wednesday night. As I took my nightly stroll I heard screaming children and the shouts of adult voices as the children were being bathed, possibly for the first time in their lives. The next morning as they walked to school, they looked a bit cleaner and many were wearing makeshift clothing: girls in skirts and dresses rolled up at the waist and belted or roped so as not to drag on the pavement and boys with shirts three times their size worn over their own threadbare pants.

Over time both the children and hosts came to a truce but the children were never really happy here in the fresh air and sunshine. They missed their street corner dice games, their familiar lives, and their parents.

Each month that passed without a bomb falling, saw more children return home to their familiar territory. Family by family came for their children and the locals here were as shocked by the parents who came to claim their children as they had been at the street urchins who arrived here at the beginning of September. Some parents did not even recognize their own children who had been cleaned up and given haircuts. From what I have heard, all the children were very happy to be returning to their former lives.

Now they are all gone with the exception of Henry and Lucy Grimes, a brother and sister who were never claimed. Their parents have not visited nor written to them for over three months. They were billeted with a middle aged brother and sister named James and Hattie Johnson, who have lived together all of their lives and took over running the family grocery when their father died. All four seem very happy with the arrangement.

I have registered our food ration books with James at Johnson's Grocery. Rationing has begun on bacon, butter and sugar. The disadvantage of living on an island is that nearly all of our supplies must be imported and, even though we have not yet seen the bombs fall, the war at sea has certainly begun. Back on the 29th of September, every householder turned in a form giving details of who lived at that address. These forms were used to help establish the ration system, which served as a means to prevent both hoarding by customers and price gouging by merchants.

Our household schedule has changed dramatically since war was declared. Now, after he eats his supper at 7:00, Mr. Malthorpe dons his helmet, overalls and armlet and leaves to perform his duties as an Air Raid Protection Warden. Most evenings, Harriet accompanies him, which is very unusual for a woman.

Please take care and write soon. Your letters are such a gift.

Love to all of you,
Your cousin Moira

*****

February 28. 1940

Dearest Moira,

Our Christmas was ever so jolly; the children created an aura of wonder and delight. It snowed on Christmas Eve, adding to the gaiety of the season. We attended an early morning service and had a lovely dinner with friends from the newspaper office and their families. There are four families with whom we are particularly close. Often we rotate entertaining for Christmas dinner. With Yoshi gone I was glad that it was not our turn to have all at our home.

Charles and I attended the wedding of a friend, Dorothy Darby, on New Year's Eve day. The ceremony was held at St. John's Episcopal Cathedral, which by the way is absolutely magnificent. The organ has over 4,000 pipes! Dorothy wore a lovely dress of Windsor blue. I thought of you, imagining how wonderful that color would look on you!

Yoshi is back with us. She arrived here around the 10th of January. The poor girl is noticeably stressed; she has lost at least ten pounds. She was tiny to begin with, so the weight loss is extreme. Her family was relieved to have Haruki released from jail, but now they do not know where he is. Once he was released, he vanished. I believe Yoshi has heard from him though, as mail has been delivered to her from someone other than her parents. No return address is on the envelope, so I can only assume that the sender is someone who does not want his/her location known.

Charles tells me that his colleagues in Washington D.C. have heard that there is speculation that our Congress will soon be addressing the "issue" of Japanese-Americans. He says that there are rumors that they will have to register as aliens, even though they have lived in this country since birth or at the very least for many years. Imagine how registering as aliens will feel to Yoshi and her brother, who were both born here!

I have read your letter to the boys; not when Catherine was present, however. There is "war talk" at school (little pitchers have big ears; the boys and their classmates only repeat what they hear at home), so I believe they should hear accurate information. Of course, the boys are most interested in the children evacuees' baths! I'm certain they have retold the story at school. I wonder from where their teachers think they get their information. At the moment, I do not think that they are frightened, but with children, and especially with male children, you can never be quite certain of what they may fear until the fear itself has taken hold. Charles spends a great deal of time with the boys answering their questions. I'm thankful that there are two of us and that no nightmares have occurred.

A 30-car train carrying regular troops from Fort George Wright, which is adjacent to our city, left last week for the Fort Lewis Army Post, which is about fifty miles south of Seattle. After two weeks the troops will proceed to Monterey, California, to continue their war games activities. Reserve Units will maintain Fort Wright. We don't know whether that will involve Charles' unit.

Entire families now live on the Post without the heads of their families. Most of the wives are very young women without much education. Fortunately, there is health care on Post; but it's not that which worries me; it's the children without fathers.

Harriet accompanies her husband on his Air Raid Protection rounds, but she did nothing to help with the children? How odd? The change in the habits of your employers is interesting to note. If you are friendly with the vicar's wife perhaps you could arrange to have tea with her on a day when *she* is managing the shop. Have you been into the shop's "backrooms"? I think that it would be interesting to see what lies behind the scene! There must be a spot in the back where the two of you can visit and have a cup of tea and some delicious treat you might bring. If she should have a customer, you could entertain yourself with a "book," or a quick look around, until she returns.

You did not mention Wills in your last letter. Is he a warden as well? You know, my darling cousin, if Harriet can accompany her husband on his rounds, why couldn't you accompany Wills on his? You might find it enlightening!

With love and wishes for your safety,

Cousin Margaret

*****

May 26, 1940

Dearest Margaret,

Your Christmas celebration sounds beautiful and uplifting. I have never seen deep snow, though I have experienced the beauty that an inch of snow brings to familiar objects before it disappears in the afternoon. I am pleased that your children enjoyed the stories of our evacuees. Thoughts of them brighten my days.

I am also pleased to hear that Yoshi has returned but am concerned about the Japanese issue arising in your country. There are similarities between Germany and Japan. Like Germany, Japan is expanding. In 1931, it began taking over Manchuria. There are other connections between those two countries as well; they both signed an anti-communist pact in 1936.

On May 10, Neville Chamberlain resigned, Winston Churchill was selected by the cabinet and the King to assume the position of prime minister and the Battle of France began when the Germans drove their tanks through the hilly, forested Ardennes in Belgium, surprised the French and occupied Northern France. These are very frightening times.

But, oh! The most amazing thing has happened. Mrs. Brown, who has lived across the street for many years, has let her house. Her son, Neville, joined up to defend our country and she, therefore, moved into the countryside to live with her younger sister Clotilde to help her run the family farm.

Robert Gentry, a most amazing man, now lives in the house. He is very interested in me and makes me feel and act like a young girl. Margaret, I have never felt like this in my life. It is as if my mind and body have become strangers to me. I find myself writing his initials in the air and on the furniture before I dust. My mind is constantly thinking of him. I, who have never paid much attention to the street in front of this house, find myself constantly looking through the sitting room window to check if his curtains have moved or whether or not his door is ajar. I now spend a great deal of time in the front garden, which will benefit us all when my crop bears fruit.

I have had my hair cut in a more modern and easy-to-care-for style and, when I go out on nippy days, I have taken to wearing one of two beautiful scarves that once belonged to my mother. For the first time, I have wished that I had bought some of those nylon hose when they were available. Until now I never thought twice about wearing my plain cottons.

Feeling like a schoolgirl is not terribly comfortable for me, but I am bewitched. Never have I received such attention from a man. Wills and I remain great friends and have a warm regard for one another. We enjoy a level of trust and friendship that I treasure. We have kept up a correspondence since he left to join the Royal Air Force. His mechanical skills are much in demand during this time of war. Since I am able to drive, he left me in charge of his lorry. Well, actually, there are two lorries but only enough parts to keep one running at a time. I imagine that the need for me to drive will only grow as more men leave and the war progresses. So far I have only been asked to haul two loads of sand. Since the lorries are signed to me, I receive enough petrol coupons to keep them running.

However, this situation with Robert is completely different and irrational. When I was growing up men were in short supply due to the number of Great War casualties and deaths from the influenza epidemic. He takes me to lunch at Tilly's Restaurant and asks all about my life. I answer him as truthfully as I can but there really is not much to tell. I certainly do not tell him about the most interesting part of my life, which is you and your family. It would have been better to meet R.G. when I was a schoolgirl. I could have shared my infatuation and giggled with the other girls.

Despite my silliness, alarms go off in my head when he asks about my employers. I do answer him truthfully from what I see. I share none of the questions that you and I are pondering. He is so tall and handsome with his dark hair, broad shoulders, midnight blue eyes behind thick glasses, and a smile that invites you into his world with no reservations.

I also question him and he seems to answer my questions with the same basic facts that I do his. He tells me that he is here to facilitate the moving of goods throughout the country, and gives me the impression that he is doing so for the government. I am amazed at how much time we can spend merely talking without really saying anything. If nothing else, I am beginning to understand some of the women characters in the books I have read. Until now, I understood nothing about the happy haze that one falls into when under the spell of an appealing man.

He registered with Johnson the Grocer and likes to accompany me as I do my daily shopping. He walks to church with me and stays after the Sunday service to talk with Vicar Dimblebey and his wife. He has an insatiable appetite for information about all of our neighbors. I find this unusual in a man. Most men discuss the war or the horses and leave the day-to-day gossip to the women.

I do not even care that people see that we are walking out together. How wonderful to feel as though I am floating on a cloud. The days go by so quickly and nothing seems like hard work. I wonder how long he will stay and wonder what life will be like without him.

Oh, dear cousin, if you were only nearby so that I could talk with you and hear your perspective. I miss you more than ever.

Please give my greetings to all your loved ones.

Much love,

Your silly schoolgirl cousin,

Moira

*****

September 18, 1940

My Dear Moira,

I wonder what has transpired between you and Robert in the three months since last you wrote. I am amused by your assessment of the gentleman. I don't think I have ever heard you so enthused about anything as much as you are about this man! You deserve all the happiness and giddiness that your relationship has produced. There is so much havoc and uncertainty in England and the world at this moment that no one can begrudge you whatever joy you find in the "gentleman across the street".

So you have bobbed your hair! How brave; I think that it's about time that I became as daring!

As for nylon hose, they are definitely hard to come by! Do you dare wear trousers? I have found them extremely comfortable, not to mention much easier in which to work. I enjoy wearing them on cooler days particularly when the furnace in the

Clinic seems in need of stoking!! I suspect you have some longer skirts you could convert into a stylish pair; the wider the leg, the less drastic the style will look.

I don't want to burst your bubble, but be wise in what you divulge to anyone. Do you not wonder why Robert has not gone off to defend the Crown? Just a thought: if he is reaping more information than you are given in return; give thought as to why! You wonder how long he will stay in Brackham Wood. Ask him!!

Bad news seems to be an every day occurrence. Norway and Denmark have been invaded; France has fallen; Romania has sided with the Nazis; Sweden has been encircled and forced to allow passage to German troops. When will it end? Or, worse yet, when will the United States become involved? The Selective Service Act was enacted this week (September 16). This is the first peacetime conscription in U.S. history. It means that all men between 21 and 35 are required to register with local draft boards. Charles and I believe that our entrance into war cannot be far behind.

With regard to Yoshi and her family: U.S.-Japanese relations are tenuous at best. Some Americans feel that many Japanese living in the U.S. are really spies for Japan. In fact, they believe that all Japanese are suspect.

In the time since the early 1900's when the Japanese were free to move to the U.S. mainland, they have prospered and are no longer low-paid workers. They are managers of farms, fishermen who own their boats, and shopkeepers with small stores and other businesses. That success has brought complaints from agricultural interests who want to eliminate them as competition.

Having a brother protesting in downtown Seattle doesn't help matters for Yoshi's family. There is still no word on Haruki's whereabouts; although a recent letter addressed to Yoshi, which arrived in our mailbox, had a Canadian postmark.

Do you remember my references to Sarah Feingold? She became my patient a couple of years ago. Her father, in three short years, has managed to purchase a piece of real estate, which also has a warehouse of considerable size. It is near the Spokane River but has not been in use for many years, so Sarah tells me. Apparently, he was able to negotiate the sale for a song. At any rate, he is now producing bread and crackers there and doing very well. He even has a truck that makes deliveries to shopkeepers. He also allows customers to purchase baked goods in an area at the front of the warehouse. Sarah quit her job at Shriners Hospital and her father has employed her to run the bakery portion of his business as well as to keep his books. She is a very smart young woman and seems to be very happy with the arrangement. The only update on Sarah's uncles, who disappeared in 1937, is that they are somewhere in Poland. My thoughts on that are of fear for their safety.

And then fear brings me back to you. Were you able to get a look at the back of the "shop"? You mentioned the Vicar and his wife, but no update on what is going on with George and Harriet. Do tell! Have you mentioned their strange behavior to Robert? I am full of questions and have no answers. Please write soon and tell me everything!

With love and worry,

Margaret

*****

October 11, 1940

My Dearest Margaret,

I was so very happy to hear from you. Now that we are immersed into the war, there is always a concern that our messages may not get through. I am answering quickly as I don't know what will happen next.

There is no more phony war; we are heavily engaged in the real thing. The Battle of Britain has begun. While Brackham Wood is not a German target, there is much air activity as the German airplanes fly over on their way to London. Anti-aircraft guns and our brave pilots occasionally bring down aircraft as they fly overhead. When a Messerschmitt plummets to the ground, it is met with the cheers of the locals. The occasional German pilot returning home with a bomb still in the bay will sometimes drop it above our village before he flies over the channel. We also see barrage balloons go up in flames.

One bomb actually hit quite near here on Mrs. Minstock's farm, which she is now running with three Land Girls who have come from London to get out of the city and help on a farm. Luckily, it landed a far distance away from the house and outbuildings but it did ruin a recently plowed field.

We live with constant air raid warnings that cause the shopkeepers to close their shops, and everyone to run to shelter. Our neighborhood shelter is a Nissen Hut constructed for and used during the last war. The council of the village of Brackham Wood claimed the hut and reconstructed it for use by the local Boy Scout Troop. The semi-circular tube, created from corrugated steel, now makes a good air raid shelter for the same reason that it made good barracks during the last war. It is inexpensive and strong, especially when fortified with sandbags, as is our shelter.

However, my dear cousin, I must confess to you that I hate that shelter. Its sounds and smells overwhelm me. It had served the community well as a scout hut, where noise didn't matter. But now the voices of whining children, arguing couples and gossiping women mix and magnify and bounce off the semicircular walls during the hours and minutes between the 'take cover' and the 'all clear' sirens. Some days I think that I will not survive hearing "Run, Rabbit, Run" sung one more time. I am happy for the posters on the entryway wall that proclaim that smoking in the shelter is strictly forbidden and remind us that dogs are not to be admitted. The air and noise would be even worse with smoke and barking.

Whenever fifty people share an enclosed space for any length of time, sanitary facilities are necessary. Ours is a chemical lav or 'Elsen Bucket' surrounded by a curtain hung from a suspended rod. The square white bucket, topped with a wooden seat and lid is filled with phenol, which sanitizes, but does nothing to deodorize the waste. A washbasin and bucket of water stand just outside the curtain.

Thank you, Margaret dear, for reading this emotional tirade. I daren't talk to anyone here in such a way. It is considered nearly traitorous to meet the problems of war with anything but a happy disposition. I really do try to remain cheerful and obey the red and white poster that proclaims: "Your courage, your cheerfulness, your resolution WILL BRING US VICTORY."

I still work with the Women's Voluntary Service (WVS) one afternoon a week. We have opened a shop that allows us to exchange and share clothing and household goods that we no longer need. We are doing our best to conserve precious resources. I rather enjoy talking with the other volunteers and helping set displays.

In addition, on some weekends I drive Wills' lorry when supplies and goods need to be moved about town or hauled to or from a railway station. Since virtually all men between 18 and 41 years of age have been conscripted and some even younger have lied about their ages and volunteered, older schoolboys and strong women and girls help me empty and fill the lorry.

I have taken your advice and now wear trousers when I work with the lorry. However, I am afraid that, rather than good-looking attire, they are very unstylish overalls. Nonetheless, I am glad for the nudge you gave me. They make it much easier to climb on and off the lorry and perform some basic maintenance. Other women are following suit as they take on the chores formerly done by men.

You asked about my visit to Mr. Malthorpe's shop. I took your advice on Friday, the 20th of last month when Mrs. Dimblebey was minding the haberdashery; I stopped in to check with her on the church flower rotation, which we call the 'rota.'

Now that we are at war, the fierce rivalry to supply the altar with the most beautiful bouquets has calmed down. Gardens have been modified as we 'Dig for Victory.' Our produce is becoming more and more important as additional items are added to our list of rationed food. In July, tea and margarine were added to the list. Each time new items are rationed, we who cook must readjust our habits and experiment with new foods. I have it easier than most because I have ration cards for three adults and, as I have mentioned, the Malthorpes are not fussy about their meals. I feel for those with growing children, who must keep them nourished with less and less food.

Back to my visit with Patricia Dimblebey—I was reminded of one Christmas holiday when George told of how much he had enjoyed spending time in the back of his father's shop when he was a child. I can now appreciate his comment. Mrs. D. asked me to join her for a cup of tea in the back room, leaving the door to the shop ajar lest any customers enter. I had a good look round as the gas ring heated the kettle to boiling.

I understood why George became fond of the back of the shop. He described being fascinated by the 56 dark oak cubbyholes above his father's combination workbench and desk. Each had held a different color or size of a piece of men's furnishings.

Few customers disturbed Patricia Dimblebey during our time in the back of the shop, but I was able to get a good look round the room when Mrs. Smith, a particularly loquacious customer, talked on and on. Underneath the workbench, I glimpsed a set of slots, each of which appeared to hold size A4 paper, used for business stationery. The metal frames above each slot *were* empty. They once, no doubt, held labels.

The only unusual feature of the back room sat above my head. A wall built of lighter and lower quality wood enclosed the three-foot space between the top of the cubbyhole cabinet and the ceiling. A finger-sized notch at the bottom of the wall allowed me to look within. All I had seen was a red light before I heard Patricia's footsteps and rapidly dismounted the chair on which I had been standing. The light reminded me of the light on the wireless that sat in the parlor or the kitchen in the homes of some of my previous employers.

This letter is becoming very long but I am sure that you would not forgive me if I did not mention my dear Robert. He still lives across the street and we spend as much time together as possible. My weeks fill up quickly with caring for the Malthorpe home, making do with the new austerity, spending time in the air raid shelter, WVS activities, and occasional work with the lorry. Robert's work often takes him away for part of a week but we try to reserve Sundays to be together.

He is not eligible to serve in the military because of his eyesight. His spectacles are extremely thick and I notice that he holds both the Book of Common Prayer and the Hymnal quite close to his eyes during Sunday Service. Even though he works in supply, I suspect that his real job has something to do with information gathering.

I am beginning to think that the U.S. is our only hope. Bombing has disabled much of our manufacturing. We have lost some of our most promising young men. Our food, supplies, and equipment are greatly diminished. Our airplanes are being destroyed faster than we can replace them. The picture looks bleak indeed.

I promise you that I will do everything I can to keep myself out of harm's way. It is heartening that someone cares.

Please give my love to all including Auntie and Uncle.

Special love to you my beloved cousin,
Moira

*****

February 7, 1941

My Dear Moira,

I have just reread your letter written in October. It is now early February, a new year, and I am wondering with the way your world is spinning whether you will receive my very late reply.

It makes me so sad to be sending you more bad news when you have so much with which to struggle. You really don't need more. But you must be told what has kept me from writing sooner. I know this will come as a terrible shock and I'm so sorry to have to be the bearer of such news.

We have lost Mummy and Father. They were killed instantly on 10 January in Chicago when their car slid on an icy road and rolled over several times.

They had been with friends for the evening and were returning home. I suppose Father shouldn't have been still driving at his age, but their friends live only a mile away. Who would have thought that such a short trip could result in losing both of them?

It is thought that Father lost control of the car which spun several times, rolling over a hillside and down the embankment to the frozen river's edge.

We all went to Chicago by train. Charles and the children stayed until after the funeral. We had only one service and buried them side-by-side the same day. My family then returned to Spokane where all were cared for primarily by Yoshi, but also by a woman from our church who Charles had hired to cook for them. At least Yoshi was a familiar face to greet the children when they came home from school. Charles soldiered on, managing to keep everyone going in the proper direction, until I could get things somewhat settled with Mummy and

Father's estate. I stayed on an additional three weeks. How I missed my darlings! We will have to return to Chicago to finalize matters when the weather improves, perhaps in May.

I didn't respond to your October letter promptly as Mummy and Father were here for the holidays; both Thanksgiving and Christmas. I'm so glad that we had that time with them. I was pleased to see how healthy they both looked. Father was not involved with any speaking engagements and had retired, unbeknownst to us, in October before coming here.

We had many evenings for family activities. We played games, read to one another, listened to the radio, and took walks in the snow. It was lovely.... just like when WE were children.

One evening, Father took us to the Davenport Hotel for dinner. Father insisted that we take Yoshi as well. It was a memorable evening for everyone! The lobby of the hotel is spectacular, but on this particular evening, so was the music. Two very young girls were playing the grand piano on the mezzanine for the guests to enjoy. Their ability was absolutely amazing. We were told that they were the daughters of Louis Davenport's secretary. Our children were in as much awe as we.

I admit that I have been so distracted and perhaps somewhat depressed with the deaths of Father and Mummy, that I've had little or no time for much else other than seeing that the children are taken care of and going to work in somewhat of a daze.

Charles has been a darling but, he too, has had little extra time to spend at home. The news business hasn't slowed a moment what with the war escalating with every tick of the clock. He rarely gets home before eight. The children are already in bed and then he is off again before six in the morning. Catherine recently asked whether Papa "still lives here."

I saw Sarah last week and she could talk about nothing but "concentration camps." We've heard snippets about these camps since 1933, but the references were always with regard to enemies of the State and in particular, the media. She was trying to convince me that the Nazis were literally "rounding up" thousands of Jews. Charles says he has only heard about "work" camps. But he says he has heard nothing about the Jewish people being incarcerated in them. I wonder where Sarah gets her information.

Now to your news…I wish more than ever that we had devised a plan to get you out of England. Your life terrifies me. Our country believes that nothing like what you are experiencing will ever touch our shores. In fact, I doubt very much if people here know half the horror that I know. No one wants to go to war. I suppose there are others in this country who have family abroad and know what I know, but for the most part citizens avoid the subject even when it is spread over the front page of their newspapers morning and night.

Our papers talk of the war in Europe, but the articles are not nearly as descriptive as yours regarding life in a bomb shelter. The sanitary conditions horrify me. I can only imagine the stress produced by living any amount of time in a situation as you described it.

Our neighbors' son recently graduated from Law School and has now gone off to Harvard for training as a Signal Corps officer. Other friends' sons have also left college to begin flight training. They have been advised to do the early training in order to get a preferred assignment. In my opinion, it won't take much more to encourage others to follow suit. Those who continue to keep their heads in the sand are going to be rudely awakened some morning!

I imagine your foray into the backroom of the haberdashery was an exciting adventure; rather like a *Nancy Drew* mystery scenario. Are you familiar with these books? They were introduced in 1930; a female version of the *Hardy Boys* mystery series. My boys love to read the latter; I can hardly wait for Catherine to be old enough to enjoy 'Nancy.' Now I'm off track...that seems to be the story of my life these days! I would love to have been your shadow as you got a look at the back of the shop. The red light, of which you spoke, the one you saw above the cubbies, might have been something electric. Could it have been a steamer for the hats George sells? Could it have been a fuse box? I'm guessing a radio, just as you think it is.

Before I close, I must ask you, yet again, to be very careful.

With much love and thoughts for your safety,
Margaret

*****

April 7, 1941

My Dearest Margaret,

How can I express my sadness and sympathy in words? I hope that by the time you receive this letter, you and your family are beginning to recover from the shock. I apologize for not responding more immediately but I was literally struck dumb by the news. As I mourned with you, I was filled with my own memories of Aunt Elizabeth and Uncle Basil. The time before you left in 1912, remains the happiest part of my life. We were so often together as one family, celebrating holidays and spending many hours in one or the other of our homes each weekend. I had no idea how the emigration of you and your parents was to change my life.

My childhood ended with your departure. Without loving Aunt Elizabeth and dear Uncle Basil our social life as a family did not exist. My mother, left to her own devices, never invited anyone into our home and we, in turn, were never asked into the homes of others. Father became so busy with his practice as a country doctor that he was tired and preoccupied when he was with us. He constantly talked of his regret at not joining his brother in America.

Oh how I wish that I had found your address and contacted you immediately after my own parents passed away. I must, however, realize that I was in such shock and terror that I had no thoughts at all. Were it not for the good women at Charwell Girls' School, I still have no idea what would have become of me.

In our correspondence over the past four years, I have dreamed of coming to the United States and visiting with you and your own family and my dear Aunt and Uncle. Since that part of my dream has been dashed, I vow that if I live through this war, I shall see you once again and meet your wonderful family.

I can only imagine your own feelings upon hearing the news. As I tend to do when reacting to tragedy, I grasp for something positive lest I drown in sorrow. I am so very glad that you were able to celebrate your parents' last holidays in such a glorious way. And I admire the strength that you demonstrated as you remained in Chicago to see to their personal affairs, even though it separated you from your husband and children when you most needed to be with them. Will your mother's cousin, Gillian, now come to live with you?

Even though I know that days are lengthening at this time of year, darkness seems to be everywhere; not only must all headlights be hooded and torches required to be turned on and off at five second intervals but electrical signs and streetlights are all now turned off at dusk. This last measure makes only a small difference in our village but has caused drastic changes to London and seaside towns like Worthing and Brighton with their formerly lighted piers and amusement arcades.

You might imagine that I am writing this letter while sitting comfortably at a desk, but I am not. I am sitting cross-legged under the Malthorpe's sturdy kitchen table wrapped in the blankets and the counterpane that I have once again dragged from my upstairs bedroom. This is now my air raid shelter even though we are told that an understairs cupboard is the safest place in the house. However, only here do I feel safe enough to read or write. I can sleep easily here except when droning aircraft fly directly overhead. When Mrs. Malthorpe does not join her husband in his duties as Air Raid Warden, she chooses to sequester herself in her upstairs bedroom during the raids.

The kitchen clock now reads a little after 2:00. The Germans quickly discovered that sending their Messerschmitts over the English Channel in the daytime was counterproductive. The British spitfires and anti-aircraft guns made quick work of the first few that flew over in daylight. Recently they seem to restrict their operations to night raids.

This warm dark kitchen has become my sanctuary, even though I found it dismal when I first moved into this house. When the sirens ring 'alarm,' I make certain that the blackout curtains cover the window. I then close the kitchen door and, by lighting a lamp, create a private reading area. No light leaks out to help German pilots find their way to London. However, unfortunately, they seem to reach their targets without my help.

At other times I put myself to sleep by visualizing the war posters that seem to cover every available space in town. Some have to do with the conserving of resources. One red poster with white lettering reads "Use It Up, Wear It Out, Make Do, Or Do Without." Another pictures a fashionable woman looking through her closet. It states, "Go through Your Wardrobe and Make Do and Mend." The one that most strongly draws my attention pictures a hefty right hand bearing a swastika ring while working a jigsaw puzzle. Above it sits the words: "Bits of Careless Talk Are Pieced Together by the Enemy."

There is scarcely any talk in this house. Only rarely do I hear anything that I could interpret to help me understand the work of George and Harriet. However, my driving skills, which I thank you for encouraging me to acquire, are becoming more and more valuable to this community as well as to understanding Harriet Malthorpe.

Only weeks ago, on March 11, the Lend-Lease Act was signed by your President Roosevelt. Since then, more and more sealed crates are arriving via railway. Each of them needs to be delivered to a specific location. Most are very heavy items, which are loaded onto my lorry along with a set of directions to their destination. These places would be hard for someone not born and raised here to locate with all the road signs removed and only local references used to denote certain areas. Lately, I have often followed directions to nowhere only to find that a complex has sprung up instantly in that place.

I imagine that this work could be dangerous for me but I no longer care. Surrounded with death, I have become inured to it. My war driving has answered some questions about my employer as well. On two or three occasions when driving my lorry near the coast, I have seen Harriet atop a hillside moving her arms in what appears to be a dance or routine as Wills had mentioned seeing before he joined up. I now suspect that she is sending signals. I only wonder to whom she is sending the message.

Oh, lest I fail to mention it, Robert has been away for two weeks. He now often leaves for two or three days, always taking the overnight bag that otherwise sits in his entry hall and saying goodbye to me. He never says where he is going and I never ask. When I saw Susan Brown, his landlady, I asked her if he had moved. She was certain that he had not because only recently had he paid rent for the upcoming three months.

Together, she and I walked to his house and, receiving no answer from her knock, Mrs. Brown used her key to open the door. The house was in good order. His overnight bag was not in the front hall and the icebox held a bit of cheese and fruitcake. His wardrobe was full. The house was left just as it would have been had he been going on a two day journey. I am keeping a close watch on the house, hoping to see him arrive there soon.

Please give my love to your family,
Your loving cousin,
Moira

*****

April 30, 1941

My Dear Cousin Moira,
    Thank you so much for your lovely letter and beautiful thoughts. Mother and Father were so glad that we had found each other once again and they were always happy when they received a letter from you. It meant so much to them to know that they were remembered with such fondness. They dearly loved your descriptions of their homeland and were so impressed by your spunkiness.
    It has been a difficult three months as you can imagine. We miss the phone calls and cards, and of course, their weekly letters. Knowing that we shall never see them again is so painful.
    Once school dismisses for the summer, we shall return to Chicago and finalize all estate business. Charles will have to return home to Spokane after only a week, as he cannot afford to take any more time away from his desk. I expect it will take me at least a month to complete everything.
    Our plan is to have Gillian remain in the house. Of course, it is too large for her to be rambling about in alone, so we have decided that she will move to the portion of the house in which Mummy and Father had lived and will rent out her rooms as well as the other two bedrooms. We registered the spaces with the medical school and already have rent applications for the coming school year. Gillian

is looking for a housekeeper/cook as I write this! Are you wondering why? This may surprise you as much as it did me.

She was very lonely once I left Chicago after the funerals. I suggested that she look for some sort of temporary work. She did just that. In fact, she found a fulltime job, albeit swing shift, as a security officer for an airplane manufacturing company in Evanston, a suburb of Chicago. I can't imagine her doing that kind of work any more than I can imagine you driving a supply-filled lorry through the countryside; but it's a different world now. She is thrilled to be so independent. The prospect of managing the care of the house and fulltime job isn't daunting at all, it seems! She's over the moon to think that she, who once cared for Mummy and Father, is now the mistress of the house.

I say "cared for" but in reality, she was more of a niece/companion to both. Once her parents were gone, she found that she had nothing but time on her hands. She had been left a small inheritance, but not enough to sustain her through her lifetime. Gillian had some secretarial training, I think perhaps a couple of years, but when her parents both became invalids at about the same time, she gave up hope of completing school and simply cared for them until their deaths. Mummy and Father traveled frequently and rambled about in that house. They offered her rooms in their home. Father "employed" her to manage his speaking engagements and his paper work. She ate meals with them, shopped with Mummy occasionally, and worked on Father's projects when necessary. She managed the house when they were gone and lived her own life when not otherwise involved with them.

I'm delighted to be able to keep the house under her care without having to rush to dispose of it.

Gillian's work involves monitoring employees who are on the factory floor, building transport aircrafts. She knows nothing about aircraft production itself, but that is apparently not necessary. Her job is to track the employees' movements. She has an uncanny skill of reading a person's intentions and watching for activity that is out of the ordinary. There is much concern about subterfuge and sabotage and since there are not enough men to fill the security positions, many women are finding this kind of work available to them.

The guards do not even have uniforms; they've been waiting two months for them to arrive. In the meantime, Gillian wears her own clothing to work. How she could ever track down a suspect in pumps, I'll never know!

I find myself overwhelmed by descriptions of your days and nights. I cannot fathom spending a night on the kitchen floor under a table. But I admire your pluckiness and bravery and I wish there were something that I could do to make this all go away for you and your countrymen, my countrymen.

Our papers scream with articles and photos of war. There is very little local news for which the citizens really have any interest. The fear that war is just around the corner is evidenced by the concerns I hear from my patients and the sermons we all hear in our various churches. We hear it at work, teas, and on the very streets. Our government has not stated that the U.S. is going to war; it's just that there are so many signs of preparation to do so.

Interesting military maneuvers have occurred here in the last few weeks. One of them is that the Army Air Corps has taken over the newly completed Sunset Field. The field was to have been a civilian airport. We suspected this would happen eventually as the Federal government has been involved in the funding of the project. Felts Field, once again, has become home to not only our civilian airfield, but it also now serves as a training facility for the Women's Army Air Corps. Most of the women are photo lab technicians. The unusual aspect is that this is one of the first sites for the training of females.

Fort George Wright, the small military post just outside the city limits, has also been building up personnel. It would seem that it is only a matter of time until something will happen.

The months since the loss of Father and Mummy have been unbelievably lonely. Even before their deaths, Charles was gone frequently for extended periods of time. I have no siblings with whom to share the grief of losing parents. Walking seems to somewhat calm my feelings of despair. In fact, I have initiated a walking program at the Clinic and have prescribed it for several of my patients as a means of weight loss and stress reduction. I have several pregnant patients who are emotional wrecks. They have other children, absent husbands, money problems, or any other multitude of worries. A long walk, which can be done with children in tow, seems to offer some comfort.

I have also convinced Charles that we should purchase a summer home; rather a place of solace where he and I and the children can reflect, refresh, and enjoy the company of one another. Charles agrees wholeheartedly and, since I have an inheritance of sorts and the cost will not completely destroy our attempts to budget, he has encouraged me to begin looking for a piece of property. I want something rustic and close enough to the city that we are able to get to and from our jobs in a relatively short period of time. I will be looking at Newman Lake and Liberty Lake which both fit that description. If we find something before school dismisses we can have any work that needs to be done, completed while we are in Chicago. I have a reliable handyman who can oversee the work during the week that Charles is with us and then he and Charles can tend to any decisions that need to be made before I return with the children.

Sometimes Yoshi goes on walks with us, but most of the time, she remains at home studying diligently, as this is her final year of school. She will be taking her last set of exams next month. She is unsure of her future but wishes to remain in Spokane as the attitude toward Japanese in Seattle at this time is extremely disturbing. The chance of finding work there may be better, but it is only a "chance" even in the area that is inhabited mainly by Japanese. At least, if she stays here, she knows she will have work and a roof over her head until she finds something permanent. I know sooner than later she will leave us, but in the interim, I'm grateful to have her.

It seems I end every letter with the same advice and so this one will be no different. Drive carefully and stay alert to what you may see along the road as you make your deliveries. I can't understand what Harriet's hand-waving means, but it must translate to something untoward. It may be time to advise the authorities of her very strange actions. Have you told Robert?

Watch the mail for a package!
With love and best wishes for your safety and happiness,
Cousin Margaret

*****

May 26, 1941

My Dearest Margaret,

Thank you so much for your recent letter. I am glad to hear that you are returning to your own routine after the recent sadness. The story of your cousin Gillian is astounding. The world has indeed changed. It is as though men are discovering that women have talents other than housework, tatting, and perhaps dabbling at art. To be put in such a position she must be very intelligent as well as exude an aura of competence. May I be so bold as to ask her age?

I am so grateful that I followed your advice to visit London. By the end of this war it may be unrecognizable. It is possible that none of our time honored landmarks will survive.

I can certainly believe that some of your patients have become 'emotional wrecks' as you call them. The strain is unbearable. Perhaps they are lucky that they have that privilege. Here in Britain despair is not allowed. Living in a culture where we constantly hear the phrases 'keep a stiff upper lip' and 'keep your pecker up,' we are cajoled into remaining cheerful.

As I write this letter, I am once again under the table lying on my stomach, propped up by my elbows. Do you remember the hours we spent in this same position in our secret room when we were young girls? My torch points upward. Its light hits the bottom of the table and is reflected back, creating a good light for reading and writing. Only to you can I express my fears and disappointments. It is unpatriotic to behave as if anything is amiss.

For example, Janet Millican, who is our same age, lost her son Harold. He lied about his age so that he could enlist when he was but 17. In March he was killed while still in training. Yet one week after hearing this terrible news, she was back at the WVS shop, saying all the correct things and even attempting a smile. But that smile did not quite reach as far as her eyes.

Rationing has now been extended to jam but as yet there is none on tinned foods. If I, who began the war with a full larder, am struggling to feed the three of us on the allotted rations, I cannot imagine how a mother with growing boys would be able to manage.

Speaking of children, I must thank you for the generous package that you sent to me. I suspect that Willy, Bert, and Catherine chose the contents; the nice notes from the boys and picture of your house from Catherine boosted my spirits immensely. When those sweets poured out onto the table I was delighted. Only a mother like yourself can imagine the joy of a child who has not seen a sweet in two years. Those multicolored wrapped candies keep well so I am handing them out to the village children a few at a time. Not even a king's ransom could buy sweets now.

Last spring because of the fear of invasion, many of our children from Brackham Wood were evacuated into the interior of the country. They were packed off with one pillowcase full of clothing, gas masks over their shoulders and nametags draped around their necks. It was an echo of the evacuation of the cities in 1939. However, about a third of the parents in this village braved peer pressure and governmental advice and kept their children at home. Now many of the parents who did follow the evacuation order are bringing their children home just as the Cockney parents did before Christmas of 1939. I expect that the Brackham Wood teachers will have returned and that the schools will be running at full force by the beginning of fall term.

Some days I take a few sweets with me when I go out for my daily shopping or to work at the WVS shop. I have gained the moniker 'the sweets lady.' Even when I go out without sweets, children now rush up to me to tell me about their lives, their pets, sometimes even their feelings. Occasionally they bring me a picture or a small trinket. Only yesterday, Sam Brown told me that he had found a pile of booklets in a sheep shed located in a protected area of the Downs. He has promised to bring one of the books to me. I would also like to get a good look at that shed. I plan to borrow Maggie's bike and ride through the Downs with a new goal: to see what has changed in the past two years.

I now wear my traditional clothing only for church, working at the WVS shop, or when I have a social engagement. Most days find me dressed in slacks, a warm jacket and plimsolls. If I am not gardening I am driving the lorry. I think that getting out onto the roads is very good for my spirits. I would feel much worse were I trapped within the house every day.

The church bells have been silenced since last June and I miss them terribly. After hearing them ring every fifteen minutes for my entire life, the silence has been hard to bear. Yet, I do not want to hear them now because they will be rung only in the event of a German invasion.

The air war is terrible. Even though our Hurricanes and Spitfires are rumored to be downing twice as many

German Aircraft as they are downing ours, the damage and devastation is impossible to comprehend. Hitler is trying to weaken us with constant bombardment. We fear imminent invasion.

Despite all the peer pressure to be cheerful, there are times when I fall into despair. We need help and cannot continue being bombed at this rate without severe consequences. I am encouraged that your country seems to be preparing to send more help even though I do not want you to suffer.

I have recently received two letters from Wills, each of which I have answered immediately. I know how important letters are to the soldiers in the field and am very happy to have an address at which to reach him. I try to keep my letters newsy, telling him of the adventures of his lorry and anecdotes about the town.

Robert Gentry has returned and is now one of the few men in town. No one asks him why he is not fighting. The thick lenses in his glasses answer the question before it is asked. We meet for tea when possible and still attend church together on the Sundays when he is home. We are developing a sense of camaraderie and comfort that is most consoling during these difficult times. He has shared with me that the Germans are receiving weather information that helps them plan their bombing raids. This information seems to be coming from this part of the coast. He asked me if I knew anything about it. I responded that I did not. However, it has just occurred to me that he may be interested in Harriet's dune dancing.

I have not yet mentioned my employers so I must tell you that George Malthorpe seems care worn and tired by his double shifts: one at the haberdashery and the other as an air raid warden. During bad bombing raids, he and the air wardens are on duty all night.

Harriet, by contrast, seems to be more energetic and optimistic than I have ever seen her.

I feel a bit guilty for eschewing my training and heritage and complaining profusely in this letter but must admit that it makes me feel a bit better and clears my head.

Thank you!!

Please give my love to all your family.

Your grateful and loving cousin,

Moira

*****

June 15, 1941

My Dearest Moira,

The children were dismissed for summer vacation on June 4 and we left the very next day, via rail, for Chicago. Gillian, who by the way is 40 years of age, met us at the station and we began the process of settling into life in a city where the children know no one. It has been a difficult couple of weeks and now that Charles has returned to Spokane, it is even more difficult. Please pardon my whining. In light of everything I know about what you are going through, I should be keeping "a stiff upper lip."

I have discovered a large park near the house, much like Comstock Park in Spokane. This park was not in existence when I was a young girl, but I'm certainly glad that it is there now. The fact that there is an Olympic-sized swimming pool has made it a popular destination in the Chicago heat for the children and has actually calmed their angst at being away from their friends. With Gillian's help, I do paperwork and keep appointments for the

settling of my parents' estate during the morning hours while they play together in the backyard and then all of us go to the pool for a couple of hours after lunch. I expect to be back in Spokane no later than the 4th of July.

I am especially motivated because just a few days ago, on 12 June, the Navy Reserve was called to Active Duty and I fear that the same could be true at any moment with the Army Air Corps. If that happened, Charles would be given notice. I wonder whether we would be able to get home before his unit deploys. Another concern is Bert. He complains constantly about muscle pain and headaches. In the back of my mind I fear the worst (polio?); I'm hoping that it is only growing pains and missing his father.

In March, the Department of War purchased Spokane's Sunset Field (the new civilian airfield) outright. It has become a training field for the Army Air Corps. They renamed it Geiger Field after a pioneer Army aviator. Who could possibly believe that war is not at hand?

I'm so anxious to see property for which we are negotiating. We found a cottage at Newman Lake. Charles came home from Chicago to find a seller had answered our inquiry and so the process began. Charles says the structure is anything but luxurious; but it is a place we all can enjoy; a place to be together, a place to refresh, a place without pressure.

You have read enough about me, but for this last thing. Mummy and Father left me a lovely inheritance. If I am wise, there will be plenty to send the children to college when they are ready. I want to share with you an amount that will get you out of

England and to us in Spokane, should you desire that. I will be sending a wire in July to your bank reflecting the amount. The following month, the wire will return to the prior amount I have been sending.

Your comment about plimsolls brought back many memories of our youth. I had all but forgotten the word. Here, we call them, tennies, or sneakers, or tennis shoes. I do hope they keep your feet warm!

I read the part of your letter about the children and the candy to my own children. William is already talking about how his Boy Scout troop might be able to send more sweets to you! I'm very proud of him! That too, will be a project we will undertake when we arrive home; although, I'm afraid it can't happen until school starts again and his troop begins their meetings anew.

I suspect you have found another mystery in which to be involved. Booklets in a shed, whatever are they? Is it safe for you to be in an area so remote? Perhaps Robert would enjoy the outing as well. I say this and know full well that you have already investigated Sam Brown's find! I look forward to hearing what you discovered!

The fact that the Germans know anything about the weather in England is puzzling. How could Germany be provided that information except by someone living in England? If the information originates near Brackham Wood, then who is the responsible party?

Moira, you don't think for a moment that it could be Harriet? Please Moira, be alert and please be careful. No matter how well you think you know someone, you may not know her at all!!!!

Has Robert indicated how long he will be in residence this time? I am comforted to know that you have found someone with whom to share your thoughts, fears and frustrations.

I am also gratified to hear that Wills is still alive. The thought of seventeen-year-old Harold dying in a war in which he should never have been involved, is horrifying. To think that our childhood friend may perish as well is something of which I do not want to ponder. I hope you will continue to write to him. Surely letters from home mean much to him!

I think about you daily and want you to know how much your letters and encouragement mean to me. You, who are in such danger, taking the time to write to me, at night, from under a table, by the light of a flashlight is absolutely mind-boggling!

All my love and prayers for your continued safety,

Margaret

*****

July 11, 1941

My Dearest, Dearest Margaret,

I apologize for not contacting you immediately after your last letter. I fear that emotions got the better of me for a few days. Our nearly five-year correspondence has expanded my life exponentially. Yet, not until I received word of the loss of Uncle Basil and Aunt Elizabeth and your generous decision, was I able to face my own loss and the pain of giving up my home, my schooling and my childhood dream of becoming a teacher in a school for girls.

I suppose that being trained to 'keep my pecker up' in other words, remain cheerful at any cost, not only helped me get to this point in life but also kept anyone in the village from noticing how badly I have felt during the past two weeks. Had anyone appeared to notice and to ask what was wrong, I would perhaps have dissolved into a puddle of tears and fallen to the pavement. I imagine it is this same training that allowed Janet Millican to return to her volunteer work so quickly after her son, Harold, was killed.

Vicar Vincent Dimblebey, aware that many of his parishioners are facing worries brought on by war, has created a prayer box. Made of simple cardboard and wrapped in green, the color of hope, the box has a large slit on the top. A pencil and small pieces of paper sit beside the box on a table to the side of the altar. I have requested prayers for all of you as well as a special separate plea for Bert's health. The Vicar prays daily for all requests and, during services, holds up the box and asks the congregation to pray together for the intentions contained therein.

Now that I look at life through your American perspective, I am amused at how uncomfortable we villagers were when the prayer box was first introduced. No one appeared to be approaching it and yet Patricia Dimblebey told me that the Vicar was constantly replenishing the paper supply. At first parishioners must have been sneaking their prayer requests into the church when it was empty. I saw no one publicly approach the box until Mrs. Minstock, the farmer, arrived early for services one Sunday, strode directly up the aisle and, with a flourish of her hand, inserted a pre-written request into the box. With the ice broken, several of us openly wrote out our requests and put them into the box after the service before we proceeded into the social hall for tea.

How delightful that William is thinking of our village children. They continue to run to me and talk when they see me in the village, which brings me much joy. However, I can imagine that they secretly hope that one day there will again be a sweet in my pocket. I still believe that, even with all of the needs created by war, these special treats give them a boost unlike anything else.

This letter is being composed in a safe and reassuring space—my Morrison Shelter. The moment I read that these shelters were available, I suggested to Mr. Malthorpe that he fill out a requisition. Since the family salary is less than 250 pounds a year, there was no cost and he took my suggestion. The shelter came very quickly. The council delivered an unbelievably heavy kit, containing 3 tools, 359 parts, and 48 nuts and bolts. Luckily, a local Boy Scout troop had volunteered to help the war effort by erecting the shelters. Since the kits were essentially giant Meccano sets, assembling them was a natural contribution for the scouts. The four corner posts were so heavy that it took two lads to carry each one into the house.

The Morrison shelter can only be described as a cage under a table. Four corner posts made of ½ inch angle iron hold up a heavy lump of 1/8 inch plate, measuring 3'6" by 6'6", which serves as the table top. Flat strips of steel are woven into a foundation for a mattress and connected to the bottom angle iron with springs, making a fairly comfortable base for my mattress. During the day the shelter serves as a tabletop. By night and during raids it becomes my territory. At first I removed the wire mesh sides when using the shelter as a table and replaced them at night. Now I leave the sides on at all times. The shelters are designed to be strong enough to protect those within even when an entire house falls upon them. Even though it is not designed to protect anyone from a direct hit by a bomb, I feel safe in mine. I never appreciated sleep until constant noise and fear robbed me of many a good night's rest.

Upon rereading your letter after emerging from my 'state,' I was reminded of the books found by Sam Brown. Though I have been deterred from checking out the site myself, Sam brought me one of the books. What a shock. The title translates into "The German Invasion Plans for the British Isles 1940." It is filled with maps, many of which are inaccurate according to RG, and many facts. I imagine that knowing that the German maps are outdated will help in defending our island. I believe that the planned invasion was postponed because of the strength of our RAF, which has not yet allowed air superiority to the Luftwaffe.

Although I have not yet digested the entire book, I will quote you a translation of the description of the English lower class:

> "they inhabit the 'slums' (homes of misery) with their poor sanitary conditions, filth, and at times morbid form of social existence (e.g. child poverty) in a state of poor health and in some cases long–term malnutrition. Some of these negative developments must be put down not to undeserved poverty but wholly or in part to insufficient competence in domestic matters, specifically among women, as well as to a lack of mutual encouragement."

I am curious as to why these books were stored here and will investigate further. In my heart I hold hopes that Hitler's decision that sent four million Axis troops to invade Russia last month assures that he will not cross the English Channel and invade our country.

Oh my dear Margaret, on my trip to Steyning today I saw the amount of my legacy. How can I ever thank you? My mind reels at the possibilities it opens to me. It is a great deal of money in the England of today.

I shall close my letter so that your mind will be relieved on the money transfer. Please accept my love, gratitude, and concern for your family.

Love forever,
Cousin Moira

*****

September 18, 1941

My Dear Moira,

I am so sorry that you have had to be alone to deal with the sadness of the last several months. It's bad enough having to go through this unhappy time at all, but worse having to do it in the middle of a war and the upheaval it brings; and then you must endure it stoically and without familial support. When I think of the years that you have had to experience such loss and loneliness, I am overwhelmed with sadness. The only thought that gives me hope is that someday, we shall meet!

That Mummy and Father are gone, and gone forever, is a daunting and devastating thought. I am constantly struggling with the reality of it. Reflecting on that, I know that at the very least, I have the support of my family. I move forward because I

must. The difference between us is that I can talk about my struggle without an askance glance, while you must keep your counsel.

My life is relatively sane and not topsy-turvy with the threat of an invasion. I sleep in a bed at night, not in a Morrison Shelter, however comforting it may be. My husband (when he's not off on assignment) and my children are at home each night with me. We are not rationing yet, although I don't doubt for a minute, that that will come in time.

Is the shelter that you call "comforting" the only one in your home? Do the Malthorpes each have one? Where are they safe if they do not?

Indeed you and your neighbors are uncomfortable in your circumstances. However, the fact that you are united in the struggle is phenomenal. There are some weeks when I never see my neighbors. Every one of them is so occupied; especially during the summer when they may be at their summer cottages for the entire three months. In the winter when we are all involved with trying to get from place to place through the snow, or removing it from our drives and sidewalks, we may call a cheery hello. It would take a calamity, I suppose, to bring us together as a community. Maybe that explains how you and your neighbors can be so close.

The books of which you spoke are very curious! Could they be propaganda? Think again about where Sam found them stored; perhaps that may give a clue as to the individuals who stored them or are about to retrieve them. Please, above all else, do not mention your findings to anyone other than Robert. Is Sam able to keep the discovery quiet? You must speak with him about that. His youth and eagerness may endanger him should it be known that it was he who made the find. Your safety is also in jeopardy now that you know of the existence of the books.

William has organized a candy collection day at his school. It is scheduled for late September. Once he and his troop have completed the drive, we will ensure that the treats are packaged and mailed to you. I hope that they will reach you in time for Christmas giving. William is so happy that such a small thing can bring so much joy. The activity is a wonderful lesson in compassion and responsibility.

Thank you for your concern about and prayers for Bert. Although he has made some improvement, a diagnosis has been made and it is indeed polio. Albeit a mild case, he is unable to walk without the assistance of braces. The fever, nausea and malaise have subsided, but he is not in school. We have hired a tutor to work with him at home until such time as he can better manage on his own. He tries to keep up with his brother, but cannot. He falls frequently and is very frustrated. Catherine, surprisingly, has been able to distract him with her pleas for help with her schoolwork and for tips on learning to ride the scooter she received for her birthday.

We spent only two weeks, in mid-August, at the cottage. Most of the work to make it livable has been completed. It was difficult for Bert to manage the trek to the dock. But he was a brave little soldier and daily would make his way with us to a sandy area of beach where he could sit and play without having to venture onto the dock. From there, minus the braces, he could be carried to the water. Fortunately, the children had swimming lessons for several years; even though his legs could not propel him, with a life jacket and his strong little arms he could maneuver about in the water just like his brother and sister. Kicking his legs was all but impossible, but it was good therapy to try. He floated confidently on his back inside the lifejacket and Charles or I would move his legs in the water. It was hard work, but a time when he felt almost untouched by the disease. A roaring fire in the winter would keep us warm enough to enjoy a couple of days at the cottage in the frigid weather. But considering Bert's condition, I doubt that we will attempt that this year.

Yoshi graduated in June and as expected has been unable to find work in Seattle. She returned to Spokane in late July and continues to care for the children. She and Catherine are sharing a room, but that is great joy to Catherine who has never liked being alone. We have space in the attic, which will be converted in a few months into a bedroom for Yoshi, a sitting area, and a smaller room, which could be used as a bedroom. She accompanied us to the lake. She was a great help for the four days when Charles wasn't there. When I wanted some time alone, I knew that the children were safe in her care. There are still letters without return addresses being sent to our home. I am convinced that they are sent from Haruki.

I now work at the Clinic four days a week. I had difficulty at first adjusting to the longer hours, but the need is great and the work rewarding. The numbers of women following the regimen of my walking program has increased, and that is validating. The newspaper even had an article about the program!

Most of the articles in the newspaper are regarding the Nazi's treatment of the Jewish population. Forcing them to wear Stars of David to identify themselves and the reported incarcerations of entire populations of cities, lends credence to the stories that Sarah Feingold told me months ago. She has become a very outspoken advocate for the city's Jewish population, which continues to bring (or attempts to bring) European Jews to this country.

There is still a racist element alive in our city, but most of the intolerance is directed at the Japanese population. They seem to confine themselves to a small area of the downtown where they live, grow vegetables in the summer, have small businesses supported by their own, or work in laundries in other parts of the city. Some like Yoshi are lucky enough to find housework or garden work in local households.

Your safety and good health remain in our thoughts and prayers.

With love,

Your concerned cousin Margaret

*****

November 13, 1941

My Dearest Margaret,

Your words of comfort have helped me a great deal. Of course, I did not like hearing that Bert has contracted polio, or infantile paralysis as we call it here. However, that he has a light case and that, as a physician you will be able to help him in every possible way, is very encouraging.

You are very perceptive to ask if each of us had a Morrison. In fact, only I felt the need of such a shelter. Mr. Malthorpe ordered it for my protection but made it very clear that neither he nor Harriet were interested in using it.

As we had hoped, Hitler's decision to turn on Russia, has offered us some surcease in the constant bombing. I have gone back to sleeping in my own bed. How wonderful to get a good night's rest uninterrupted by sirens or nightmares or Mr. Malthorpe and sometimes his wife coming in at 2:00 after a night on patrol!

Now that the constant assaults from the air have abated and I am able to sleep during the night, I am beginning to understand the horrors of war. On the rare occasions when I go to the movie theater, I take no pleasure in the newsreels that portray the destruction that we have visited upon our enemies.

Robert Gentry and I had a long and revealing talk as we walked on the Downs last Sunday afternoon. He talked quite freely of his work. While it is true that he works for the government in supply distribution, he also works for an unnamed government entity. He assured me that, since he had not signed the Official Secrets Act, he was free to talk with me about some issues that he is investigating. While I expressed surprise at his revelation I was not truly taken aback when he told me that he suspected that George and Harriet were part of a network, gathering information on possible German spies sent to facilitate the German invasion.

In preparation for the invasion, Hitler began a campaign to destroy the Royal Air Force. After nearly a month of continuous bombing of airfields, ports and factories, there seems to be a consensus, that Hitler has postponed his plans for invasion. He then began a relentless night bombing campaign to destroy the morale of the English population. We now know that that London was attacked on 57 consecutive nights and that other cities were also bombed, along with villages and towns. These attacks killed more than 40,000 of our countrymen.

However, the Battle of Britain, as it is now called did nothing but strengthen our resolve not to let the 'Jerries' take over. Perhaps that is why Hitler turned his attention to the Eastern Front. I do not, however, harbor any illusion that he has no plans for future attacks.

On my walk with Robert, I had in mind to find and retrieve the rest of the little green "German Invasion Plans for the British Isles" that Sam Brown had found in the sheep shed and give them to him. My belief that I had found the shed was confirmed when I discovered Sam's mark, a twisted version of his initials, carved into the doorjamb. However, to my amazement all the books had vanished!

Before we arrived home, Robert revealed that he was also aware that certain information was still being transferred to Germany. The communication had not ended with the passing of weather reports that had gone on during the bombing raids.

Earlier this week, I decided to give a good clean to Mr. and Mrs. Malthorpe's private room. I regularly give it a good monthly hoovering and dusting but have never before opened drawers or moved the furniture to clean underneath. The room holds two very heavy but comfortable chairs in which they sit to read of an evening. For some reason, I was motivated to move them and clean underneath. One was considerably heavier than the other, which led me to investigate. Under the platform below the cushion I found a wooden box filled with the missing green books.

The discovery of the books, along with another incident, has caused me to frame a series of uncomfortable and even frightening questions.

The second incident took place yesterday when Harriet's brother, Malcolm, paid an unplanned visit to his sister. I was quite glad to see him until the fireworks erupted. Malcolm had come to tell Harriet that he had received a visit from Monica Graves who had taught German to Harriet at the finishing school she had attended in Switzerland. Monica wished to talk with Harriet because she was disturbed about something she had witnessed when they were both at the school. Harriet reacted quite violently and she made it very clear that she was not the least bit interested in digging up old friends. The passion and vituperation in her voice was like nothing I had ever heard from her.

Suddenly the scales fell from my eyes and I saw the Malthorpes with new vision much as you have always seen them. The following questions arose in my mind: Is information being passed to Germany from one or both of the Malthorpes? What about Harriet's constant bicycle trips and her dance on the Downs? Could this be related to the strange design of the clothing that I sewed for her before war began? Could this explain her uncharacteristically happy nature as the bombing of the airfields began?

***

I continue this letter after a three-day break.

***

This missive was delayed because two days ago the afternoon post contained a letter from Wills. He is in hospital in Brighton. Upon reading the news, I made a plan to visit with him the following day. I assembled a parcel of gifts and left early the next morning for the train station where I had expected to wait for several hours until a train not filled with soldiers stopped to allow a civilian to board. Luckily my journey began earlier than I expected. The first train for Brighton had available seats.

I was in no way prepared for the Wills I was to meet. Upon reaching the hospital, I stopped to talk with matron, Sister Wilson, who expressed her gratitude that someone was there to visit Sgt. Barrow. She felt that he was badly in need of visitors, having had none in the three weeks since he arrived. She sent her assistant ahead with directions that he be prepared for a visit and directed me to the solarium where we were to meet. She then explained that he was being treated for injuries to his lower legs and feet.

As I proceeded through the hallway toward our meeting place, I thought about others who could come to visit him. Sadly, I realized that there was no one. In the village he had many acquaintances but had kept to himself since the tragic death of his wife and child. Of course, he often met with other men of the village to share a pint at the local pub but these mates were now, without exception, away from home serving in uniform.

I was barely able to suppress a gasp as the nurse wheeled him into the room. I had imagined him as I last saw him two years ago. However, his familiar even-featured face was pale and unanimated. His vibrant energy had deserted him and his broad shoulders slumped before him. Not knowing what to do, I began our conversation with the usual pleasantries. When they elicited no response from him, and, in my discomfort, I fear that I began to jabber.

Then slowly, very slowly, recognition came to his eyes. I was thrilled when at last he said my name. He did not want me to leave after my ninety-minute visit. I also wanted to stay longer but I could see that he was tiring so I left him with a promise to return next Sunday.

You were there with us in spirit during this visit. Wills expressed no interest when I spoke of our village during wartime or the difficulties that war brought to the lives of civilians. However, he brightened when I began to speak of you and your family. He began to ask all sorts of questions. We spoke of you, Charles, the children, Spokane, your lake retreat, the vast distances from place to place in your country and America in general.

He spoke not a word about his experiences in uniform and I began to understand that he needed an escape from war. During our conversation, we were both transported 3,000 miles across the Atlantic and another 3,000 across the North American continent to the West Coast. We had often talked of you during our prewar Sunday visits and, of course, he remembered you very well from our early school days together. I was careful not bring up our memory of his mother mashing his peas, carrots and potatoes together before he would eat it.

I must walk this letter to Steyning, so will close now with much love and concern for you all.

Your loving cousin,
Moira

*****

December 14, 1941

My Dearest Moira,

I fear that this letter may not reach you in light of the events of the past week; perhaps the candy

collected by William and his friends will not reach you and your dear little friends either.

Indeed, our country has changed dramatically; perhaps not in comparison to the changes in yours, but nonetheless the day has arrived that some believed never would.

After Mr. Roosevelt's Declaration of War Address to Congress on December 8, the words "a date which will live in infamy" have resounded endlessly. Our reporters are doing the best they can to make sense of what actually happened at Pearl Harbor, but information is slow at best in coming. The newspaper has Charles poised to go to Hawaii. However, civilian aircraft are not flying there at the present time and he is just waiting for permission to do so. In the meantime, journalists throughout the country try to analyze what they do know; what we have read for the past week has been virtually the same reworked information.

After President Roosevelt's address, our governor, Arthur B. Langlie, issued the following statement: "Your state government is prepared and ready to perform every defense task which has or will be assigned to it. The state of Washington is on the frontier of a great war."

That attitude is echoed by everyone with whom I have spoken. The 1500 who died and the 1500 injuries at Pearl Harbor, which were initially reported, have brought patriots to attention. Charles' Reserve unit has been placed "on alert," but thus far nothing has been mentioned about deployment. The Command has issued an order to the troops not to leave the state. Charles may or may not be exempted should he be able to get a flight to Hawaii.

A secret United States Navy radio station on Bainbridge Island's Fort Ward (just west of Seattle on Puget Sound), was rumored to have intercepted a message from Tokyo to the Japanese ambassador in Washington D.C. at 1:30 AM on December 7. The ambassador was advised to break off peace negotiations with the U.S., but its secret purpose was to alert the ambassador of the imminent attack. Apparently, delays in translating the message resulted in its delivery to the U.S. Secretary of State only 20 minutes before the actual attack began.

Fear and suspicion of Japanese Americans is running high, especially in Seattle where the Asian population is much larger than that of Spokane. There is some harassment in Spokane, even though the citizenry has been requested to "realize that the great majority of our people, including Japanese residents, are loyal to our country and it therefore is important to avoid unjust or unfounded suspicion."

You may find this as interesting as I found it unnerving. We took the children on our annual Christmas tree cutting expedition to the cottage at Newman Lake. There was about a foot-and-a-half of snow around the cottage; there were also unknown footprints. Someone had been inside and had built a fire. There was no damage to the cottage itself, but the thought that someone, whom we did not know, was in our home was most unsettling. Yoshi was with us to help with Bert. She was extremely upset and distracted with our finding. I almost wish we hadn't taken her as she was like having another child to watch! She was absolutely no help with Bert.

William listens to the radio whenever he gets the chance. Of course whatever William does, Bert must do the same. They prefer the news broadcasts to "The Quiz Kids"! I want them to be aware of what is going on in the world but at the same time not to become preoccupied with war and death and pain. It is bad enough that the children have a brother crippled by polio; it's a terrible strain on them to watch him daily struggle to gain strength to walk again. Now they must live with their country at war. I worry that their childhood is over; that they will now be forced into remembering these years with only fear.

The Malthorpes did not feel the need to order a Morrison Shelter for their own safety? How could they possibly think that they would not be targeted by German bombs?! Selective bombing; really?!

Harriet refused to talk with an acquaintance from her days at school in Switzerland? "Something is rotten in the State of Denmark," I'd say. Why would she do that?! Perhaps she has something to hide or she is afraid of Monica Graves.

You continue to play with fire and are now perhaps burning the candle at both ends, so to speak. How can Robert possibly believe that your employers are English patriots and not German spies? Have you told him about finding the books in their room? If communication with Germany has continued, then one doesn't have to look very much further than the Malthorpes as the culprits.

Poor Wills! You did very well to get him to speak at all. The horrors that he has undoubtedly seen are probably best left behind during your visits. He lives with them every moment of his days. The diversion of another place, another time, more pleasant than he has recently experienced, will be good for him. Wills will have to face the reality of what is to

become of his life soon enough. For now to have
company and to look forward to presents gives him
great comfort. It is wonderful and fortuitous that
you have the freedom from your work to travel to
Brighton.

Before I post this letter, I have a surprise. Tom
Walker, Charles' brother, is also a journalist.
Perhaps you recall my telling you about his coverage
of the King and Queen's Vancouver B.C. visit in
1939. He is a gregarious character and makes
friends very easily. Apparently, he created some
friendships while in Canada with some British
reporters who, just a few months ago, advised him
of a position for an American reporter to liaise with
the BBC. Tom received permission from his editor
and then applied for the job. He was selected for the
position! It's a sort of information sharing project
between the two media corporations. One of the
BBC's reporters will come to live in Spokane and
work for the paper here; while Tom lives and works
in London. We have no idea why the BBC would
send their reporter here rather than a large city like
New York or Chicago, but are thrilled for Thomas
to have this opportunity. This is a real feather in
Tom's cap and that of our newspaper. We are very
proud of him. He will be leaving Spokane sometime
during the next six weeks.

Would you like to meet him? If you are able get
to London or he to you in Brackham Wood, I think
you would have much about which to "jabber." He
is four years older than we and has never married.
He has a wonderful sense of humor and I think that
you would find him quite a diversion...unless of
course your relationship with Robert has grown into
something of which you've yet to speak. Just give it

some thought. Charles can always get a message to Tom through the paper, so I won't even suggest a meeting with you to him before he leaves.

I hold you in my heart and pray for your safety.
With love,
Margaret

*****

January 26, 1942

My Dear, Dear Margaret,

I am so happy that both your most welcome letter and the gift package from William arrived in time for Christmas. First I must tell you that the children in town are more than thrilled with the gifts from the American Boy Scouts. Enclosed is a letter for William to share with his troop. I believe that all the village children who are able to write have signed it. If only we had a motion picture to send you. The looks on the faces of the boys and girls as they received their small packets would warm your hearts.

Several mothers also asked me to pass on their gratitude. Until now they have always been able to provide sweets for their children at Christmas. This was the first time that it would have been impossible. They were heartbroken at the thought.

This past year jam, cheese, clothing, eggs, and coal were added to our ration list. Coal does not need to be imported but, because more and more miners have been called into the military, it, too, is in short supply. I imagine that the lack of constant bombing has made us all more conscious of the miserable conditions in which we now live. Even I am struggling to feed our three adults, two of whom are not always home.

You can see that the campaign to 'Dig for Victory' is a real help to us in these days. Were it not for homegrown food, I doubt we could survive. You can imagine that we are often hungry, particularly the children. Last April, when your country began the Lend-Lease program, one of the commodities sent was a meat product called SPAM. Even sliced very thin and fried, it helps us reach the satisfied feeling that comes only from a full stomach. Many recipes include a bit of diced Spam just to add some fat to our diet. It is actually quite tasty when fried to a crisp. Oils and fats are in short supply here, being needed for ammunition.

As to your country's entry into war, I am of two minds. Of course, I hate to see any country at war and particularly one where my family lives. I hope and pray that your distance from Europe will protect you from being attacked. On the other hand, you may remember that we were schooled to believe that "There Will Always Be an England." However, without the intervention of your country, I am not certain how long we can hold up.

Margaret, I am so sorry to hear that you found evidence of your lake home being used. How invasive! Since Yoshi was so inordinately upset, the thought occurred to me that she could, perhaps, know who was staying there. Could it possibly be her brother, Haruki? He seems to be in hiding somewhere. Perhaps he has been there for some time, always being warned when the family was coming. Did you quickly decide to go tree cutting, giving her no time to send a message? That could be one explanation of her uncharacteristic state of distraction.

I do feel for the Japanese who are being harassed. Here in Britain, Germans were hauled away from home at the beginning of the war and interned as potential enemy aliens even though there was no evidence of collusion with the enemy. Some were treated well but most of the internment locations were abominable. Most were released as the fear of invasion abated. This information is not widely known. Only through Robert did I learn of it.

I do think that the booklets I found are the same ones that Sam discovered in the shed. They were of the size, color and quantity he described.

And now, dear Margaret, do I come to the most exciting part of your letter. I must admit that the possibility of meeting Charles' brother, Tom, has lifted me out of my war doldrums. Imagine meeting a member of your family!! Of course, it is not only that but the possibility that I might find congenial companionship and perhaps even laughter. I hold high hopes for our meeting. I must not put into words how I feel just now.

Suffice it to say that my imagination is rampant with ideas for how this meeting could turn out. He must never hear that I feel this way or he would, no doubt, 'make for the hills.' I don't know if Americans use that expression but here it means escape as quickly as possible.

My relationship with Robert is now one of information exchange. I know that his interest in me gave me the giddy schoolgirl experience that I had missed when I was younger and for that I am grateful. Over time, however, I have become more realistic. His work demands that he be gone for weeks at a time with no warning when his next departure is to take place. At first I was devastated and watched eagerly, almost compulsively, for his return. Over time, however, my eagerness waned. I became aware that I was a vehicle through which he could gather information and, if his praise of me was honest, a good sounding board to help him put his observations into context.

I had no need to test my own ideas out on Robert, since you, dear cousin, serve as a check and balance to my observations. I now must tell you something that very much frightens me. I wrote you of Malcolm visiting here with the news that Monica Graves, former teacher of Harriet, had wished to see her to discuss a disturbing school memory. Just this morning, Robert told me that a woman of the same name was killed after she apparently jumped in front of a train as it was leaving the Victoria Tube Station.

Perhaps that could be a reason for me to meet and talk with a certain American journalist to discover if he knows anything about the incident. I am certain that he will be privy to information sources that may help me make sense of this incident. If, as we suspect, Harriet's identity is in question, this could be very frightening news indeed. Besides, the thought of meeting Tom is most appealing.

I have confidence that you will be able to bring up the idea of meeting me in a way that your brother-in-law will accept. I do wish to see him and also to investigate the death of poor Monica.

I shall mail this letter on the way to visit Wills. He is a little improved. According to matron, even the smallest steps are very good signs. She encourages me to come as often as possible.

Thank you again for all of your Christmas gifts both for the village children and me. I am grateful that they arrived and send this reply quickly in hopes that it, too, will reach its destination.

I send my love to you, Charles, William, Bert and Catherine.

Moira

*****

February 4, 1942

My Darling Moira,

I'm so relieved to know that you did in fact receive the candy that William and his troop sent. He was so excited to share the letter with his fellow Scouts. A photo appeared in the newspaper regarding their effort; the boys however were more excited about the badges they earned than the "silly photograph." What a good feeling it is to know that many children in a little village in England were a bit happier this Christmas because of a few Spokane, Washington Boy Scouts' efforts.

As far as rationing here: at this point nothing of real concern to the population is being rationed, other than to note that in December tires began to be rationed and after the first of January, automobile factories ceased production and switched to the production of military vehicles only. Our country has been asked to "voluntarily" ration, but I don't see much evidence of that. We've been asked to turn in old tires, rubber shoes, coats, bathing caps, hot water bottles, hoses, and even girdles as rubber is becoming more difficult to come by. The fact that the Japanese have been able to shut down exports to the U.S. from the prime rubber producing nations of Malaya and the Dutch East Indies has virtually eliminated our rubber supply. We've been asked to drive less. Charles has been taking public transportation to work, while I am still able to use our vehicle for passage to and from work at the Clinic. Otherwise, I too use public transportation. A "Victory Speed" of 35 mph has been instituted because tires wear out half as quickly at that speed, than at 60 mph. We've also been encouraged to share rides and to avoid rough roads.

I'm stewing about how we can get to the cottage under these restrictions. It may be that we will have to take the Northern Pacific train, which goes through Moab, a small town, just a few miles from the lake. I suppose at that point we could hire a wagon to take us the remainder of the way. Of course, we won't do that until spring when the roads have dried out and passage is easier.

We worry about the intruder returning. We know a family living in Moab who may be willing to drop by in their sleigh every so often. At least that way we would know whether all is well.

President Roosevelt issued an executive order, known as E.O. 9066 on February 2, which requires the expulsion of all Japanese Americans from the West Coast. A temporary assembly area is being constructed near Seattle for the 7500+ evacuees. It is called "Camp Harmony," but its description sounds nothing like harmony, rather misery. The people will stay there until they are transferred to a permanent "relocation center."

Yoshi's family has been taken to Camp Harmony. For the moment, she is safe to move at will here in Spokane. She has received no mysterious communications for the past month. I can't recall whether I gave Yoshi enough time to alert Haruki if he, indeed, is the December intruder. It is certainly a possibility and I shall watch her movements more carefully when next we go.

The news about Monica is very disturbing. Could Malcolm be involved in her death? I can't think of a motive other than to protect his sister; if she really is his sister. You are in a position of not knowing whom to trust. That makes your interest in them all the more dangerous; that's an understatement!! If Wills is improved to a degree that permits conversation of what is going on in Brackham Wood, could he be your sounding board?

I'm glad that you would like to meet Thomas. Charles will contact him with your name and address (Thomas is now on his way to London). I'm certain that it will take several weeks for him to get established before he can get away to visit you. What are the chances that you can go to him? Your thoughts and imaginings about Thomas are safe with me.

The children are well. The snow keeps them giggling and schoolwork keeps them occupied. Catherine has begun piano lessons. Bert is very much a reader; he is always happy for Saturday to arrive so he can go to the library. I allow him to stay longer than William and Catherine's dash in and dash out. Bert thrives on that little bit of independence; it is one thing he can do all by himself!

William's Scout Troop is "working" for the Office of Civilian Defense. They have been collecting aluminum and books and stand ready to do anything that a local official might deem necessary. After the 42 years of their existence, the Boy Scouts are a well-oiled machine that can get the job done.

I look forward to your letters and keep you in my heart.

With love,
Margaret

*****

March 10, 1942

My Dearest Margaret,

I am so happy to have your letter. You seem to be doing well as you adjust to the vagaries of a country at war. Camp Harmony sounds like anything but its name. I am glad to hear that you still have Yoshi with you.

I can imagine your worry about your Lake Newman property. Since so much building is going on in your area, do you suppose that you could rent it out during the months that you cannot get there? Would that help keep it from danger?

I must now tell you of the changes that have taken place within me since last I wrote. With the death of Monica Graves, all the warnings that you have sent me over the years were finally driven home. I realize that I blithely went through life, exploring my employers, checking out our house, and keeping my eyes open as I drove Wills' truck around the downs. I felt no danger. I appreciated your concerns but never really felt them.

However, I have become terrified since I learned that Miss Graves was very likely pushed in front of the train in the tube station. She was clearly bothered by something that she saw while at school in Switzerland and wanted to talk with her former pupil. Harriet was nearly hysterical when Malcolm gave her this news. Miss Graves has almost certainly been murdered. Is there a connection?

So I see my danger through your eyes and, given my own predilections, I would no doubt retreat back into the solitary state in which I lived my earlier life. I can no longer do that. I now experience a great deal of enjoyment from my interactions with the other villagers. Just now, all the talk is of what we will be planting for the coming year and sharing recipes. Even if I wanted to withdraw from village society, it would be impossible because of the length of time that we stand in lines while the grocer checks and stamps our ration booklets.

I now realize that I must watch my words very carefully and have become hyper-vigilant in my own household. I no longer purport to know who is trustworthy. My instinct is to trust George Malthorpe, Malcolm Blake and Robert Gentry. I feel that, while Harriet works with them, she possibly may also be simultaneously working for another entity.

So how did I learn that Monica Graves was likely pushed? You may have already heard that I have met Thomas in London. What a delightful man—full of laughter and fun while at the same time being intelligent and thoughtful. Because I am your cousin we felt like old friends from the first few minutes of our meeting at one of the many Lyon's Tea Shops in London. Happily, I had received a letter from him just as I was preparing for a journey.

Again I am ahead of my story. I have traveled to London as a companion to Wills as he meets with specialists to seek treatment that could be of help to him. Slight feeling is beginning to return to his feet but his muscles are very weak after such a long spell in a wheel chair. He knew that he needed to be in hospital in London for at least four days so I arranged to room and board once again with Mary Anne Withers in the same house where I stayed during my prewar visit to London. German bombs compromised many of the homes on her street during the Blitz. While her house was similarly affected, it did not suffer severe structural damage and she seems happy to have me staying with her once again.

Thomas was able to read the accounts of witnesses to the death of Monica Graves and, from their stories has concluded that she was, indeed, very likely pushed, although no one seems to have seen the perpetrator. The press is very careful to keep up the spirits of the British people. Therefore, only a limited amount of bad news actually reaches the popular press.

I have reconstructed a string of questions. Was I hired by the Malthorpes in order to make George look like the typical hometown boy coming back to live with his new wife in his inherited house? Was his marriage to Harriet merely to make an acceptable liaison for them to live together as they did their work for the British government? Does Malcolm know about their activity? Is he part of it? Was Robert Gentry sent to watch them? Is Harriet who she says she is or did she switch identities and, if so, what happened to the girl who really was Harriet? How much does George know about Harriet? However, I am much too frightened to examine any of these questions at the present time and will enjoy my stay in London.

I visit Wills when allowed but, since he is in hospital and undergoing countless examinations and a long wait is required for each of them, I have only seen him twice in the past four days. Though we had planned to remain here for only four days, we shall stay at least a week; a fact that makes me quite joyous.

Thomas has a great deal of freedom as he gets to know the city and I happily walk and ride around town with him, mostly in double-decker busses. When weather permits, we climb up the stairs to the open deck where we enjoy 360-degree views of the city. I am shocked by all the damaged buildings and quite impressed by our people, who manage to maintain their daily routines. They continue to dress in their best clothing and proceed as if nothing has happened; despite the fact that some lanes remain bordered by rubble that, until very recently, was part of neighborhood homes, shops, schools and restaurants.

I flatter myself by thinking that I am of some service to Thomas in answering his questions about typical British behavior, culture and wartime life. I do not ask about his assignment but it appears as though he is getting to know the territory.

Since he speaks slowly and articulately I have no trouble understanding his American accent. It is as if he has experience talking with foreigners. The same cannot be said of the many American soldiers who are flooding our country as I write. While walking the streets of London, we have occasionally been asked directions by these American soldiers. Thomas answers them easily and they slap him heartily on the back, glad to talk to an American on the streets. I, however, have no idea what they have said.

Putting into words my impression of the 'friendly invasion' of Americans is very difficult. First I must say that, until the Americans appeared we saw scarcely any males between the ages of 16 and 50. Those we did see were usually disabled in some way. We all suffer from scarce food rations and our clothing is becoming a bit tatty at the edges. So think of the impression made by rank on rank of marching soldiers: all fit, well dressed, well fed, large, handsome and loud as they enter a town or city.

Children and women of all ages line the streets to cheer and to look over the passing parade. When not marching in rhythm, the GIs infuse the pubs and restaurants with new money. So far they have only marched through our little town on the way to some of the bases which have arisen and to which I ferried supplies in Wills' lorry quite recently.

Being a young woman right now would be very exciting and dangerous as these well-fed, well-provisioned handsome young specimens come into town bearing gifts of chocolate and nylon stockings. They also smell different than our men. I felt bold enough to ask Thomas, who I failed to mention, is one of the handsomest of our imports, about that fact. He explained to me that they were wearing a product called 'deodorant' to keep away the odors of hard work and that after shaving, some also slap a fine smelling product called "after shave" on their faces. While I have often regretted the fact that I have no children, I must admit that I am glad not to be the mother of a teenaged daughter just now.

Even though I know that America is a much larger place and a different culture than ours, I had somehow pictured it full of English people. Silly of me, I know. All these Americans add a glamour and shine to our besieged island and I am more and more anxious to be there with you long enough to immerse myself in that culture. I must confess that I hold my head quite high as I walk around the city beside Thomas or sit beside him on the top deck of a motorbus.

He has got his hand on a booklet given to American servicemen as they arrive in Britain. I simply must copy out a few passages for you to enjoy.

According to Thomas, American servicemen are also shown films on how to behave in Britain and to understand "us." Locals who get their hands on this booklet feel quite exposed, as they are unused to seeing themselves described in such a candid manner.

As always I wish you and all of yours the very best and look forward to hearing from you soon again.

Much love,

Your cousin Moira

*****

April 27, 1942

Dearest Moira,

Just knowing that you have met Tom and that he is not far from you, gives me immeasurable peace. He has told Charles that he is entrenched with the BBC and extremely involved with his work. That would be par for Tom; he doesn't sleep until he has jumped in with both feet and is at once comfortable with whatever he is expected to do.

He has made contact with (perhaps he did it before he left the U.S.) people who are able to provide you with protection should that be necessary. He had often heard me speak of your adventures and my concerns for you. He didn't tell us what he had done until after he had arrived in London. How he can connect with governmental agencies so easily is beyond me. I'm amazed at how he manages to blend in wherever he goes. It's as if he has lived there all his life. Sometimes I think that he is not a mere journalist! I'm becoming suspicious of everyone!

I am so glad that you find him pleasant and enjoyable company. He told Charles that when he first saw you, he thought he was seeing me. That we should look alike after all these years gives me great pleasure. Thomas also said that you are a delightful conversationalist, with a ready wit and an infectious

giggle. Tom does not suffer flighty women; I think he is very taken with your charm and intelligence.

Of one thing I am certain: if you tell him of your concerns and ask him to make inquiries about Monica, he will most certainly do so. With Thomas doing the information gathering, you would be much safer than attempting to do it yourself.

You play a very important role in the defense of your country. You certainly cannot become a shrinking violet now that you recognize the danger in which you may be. You must play your role without drawing attention to yourself. You have done that well to this point. Please communicate your concerns and questions to Thomas.

It is wonderful to learn that there is progress with Wills' rehabilitation. It's also fortuitous that he goes to London for treatment!!!

Indeed, our lives in the States have changed, though not in the drastic manner in which your life changed. There is much building and what appears to be war preparation going on in the city. Fort Wright, a small military installation to the west of the city center, has become home to a number of regular and reserve army units. Basic training, marching, first aid, rifle instruction, vehicle driving, and the like seem to be the major focus of the Post. Counter-intelligence and protection from chemical warfare are also taught. In fact, every soldier is issued a gasmask.

You will not believe what I am going tell you now. Gillian has moved...west, that is. It would take me three letters to explain what prompted the move. Suffice it to say that she wanted a change of scenery and to be closer to family. We do have beautiful scenery and since I am her only family, Spokane was a natural choice.

Gillian has changed considerably since the deaths of Father and Mummy. She is no longer the quiet unassuming cousin I once knew. I suppose her job has become her life, but it also has given her a tremendous amount of experience, drive and self-confidence.

Her work experience brought her to the attention of Brown Industries, a company located just a few miles to the east of Spokane. The company has been here in some form or another since the Great Fire in 1889. In the late Twenties, they began making trailers, but by the time war was declared, they had begun manufacturing aircraft.

The company hires many women as there is a definite shortage of men. Gillian was hired as the head of security for the plant.

Without a blink of an eye, she bought a three-bedroom brick house, just a few blocks from ours. William has great plans for her yard and what he can do with what he earns working in it. He has become quite the entrepreneur!

Father and Mummy's home is now in the capable hands of a Real Estate manager, also a woman. It now is home to three interns and their families. For the moment, I am happy with that situation. It is difficult to think of selling, but it has crossed my mind. Yoshi has not seen her family since their forced removal to "Camp Harmony." The Nisei, Americans born to Japanese parents, and the Nikkei, Japanese immigrants, have suffered through a very wet spring in the Camp. The rain and the mud must be as shocking as the loss of their freedom. Nevertheless, newspapers indicate that they have set up a community of sorts. The Nisei teachers and volunteer internees work with the young detainees in a "vacation school," while other volunteers set up a rotating library with books provided by the Seattle Public Library.

Although the mail is heavily censored, Yoshi has been able to maintain contact with her parents. A letter, not from her parents but addressed to Yoshi, arrived recently. There was no return address, but the postmark was Moab. It's the village at the south end of Newman Lake. I wonder whether Yoshi has met someone who lives near Moab or, perhaps, it is from her still-missing brother.

We have plans to go to the lake in a few weeks to open the cottage for the summer. Although there is a shortage of gas and what there is, is heavily rationed, we will still be able to get to and from the cottage during the summer. It will mean, however, that Yoshi and the children will remain there by themselves for longer periods of time. Charles and I will be unable to make the drive daily as we once did. The children of course, don't mind the plan at all.

My work continues to occupy four days of the week. I am busy, but not overwhelmed.

The children are ready for summer vacation. All are well and thriving, but anxious for the school year to conclude. Bert "runs" with his friends and although always last, he continues to try to act like a normal healthy child.

Charles is very busy with work, as you can well imagine; the presses never quit. I must confess that we are very worried that his unit will be activated soon. On this I do not like to dwell.

With love and prayers for your continued safety,

Margaret

*****

June 27. 1942

Dearest Margaret,

As always I was very happy to hear from you. Your letters are a gift. I love to hear of your family and I now realize how lucky I am to have the perspective that your messages give me.

What wonderful news that Bert is improving and that his spirit is good. As I reflect on your children I am inspired by the caring relationship they seem to have. In my neighborhood, I overhear some terrible abuse passing between siblings. As an only child I imagined my siblings and I enjoying life together in a mutually supportive relationship.

I am impressed and also curious about what motivated Gillian to move 2,000 miles from her home, find a job, and buy a house. I am certain that being near family played a big part in her decision.

I wonder whether or not Yoshi's brother is somewhere near you. Is Moab a very big town? Once again I was deceived by the geography of the U.S. I had thought you lived near the Pacific Ocean but was relieved to discover that it is over 300 miles from your home.

Besides being a connection to family and a source of perspective, your letters are a gift in another way. They force me to sit down and review what has gone on in my life since I last wrote. If I were forced to describe my life since March in one word I would have to choose "unsettled." I now keep my Gladstone bag in my bedroom rather than returning it to the tiny attic storage space because I am traveling quite a bit. It is a very old bag but I am fond of it. It reminds me of the one that my father carried as he went on his house calls.

Every three weeks I accompany Wills on the train as he returns to London for two to three days of treatment. Physically he is making strides. He can now walk short distances using two sticks. He also is becoming more cheerful. I wonder how much of his cheerfulness comes from Nurse Beattie, who seems to work on all of his appointment days. June Beattie is a woman of about 30 years of age who was widowed when her home was destroyed by a direct hit during the Battle of Britain. Her 40-year-old husband had just returned after a long day's work as a chartered accountant when the bomb fell. She was still at the hospital when the tragedy occurred and returned home to the shattering sight and terrible news.

I do not mind the trips to London because they give me time to spend with Thomas, who is great fun as well as being a great comfort to me. I do so enjoy his company and also enjoy his view of the inhabitants of England. I do not know how but he seems to have gained access to some of London's exclusive men's clubs. He is amazed at the sense of entitlement of our royalty and aristocracy.

He laughed riotously when I told him the story of the 10th Duke of Marlborough who, in the 1920s, was visiting his daughter without his valet. "What is the matter with my toothbrush? The damned thing won't foam anymore." The Duke had no idea that his valet had been putting toothpaste on his brush for his entire life. Thomas is right. Servants do everything for their masters. They wash them, dress them, stay up late to help them out of their evening clothes and awaken early to prepare them for the next day.

I think I am lucky to have been a maid-of-all work to hard-working women who merely had too much to do. I helped but we were busy from sun up to sundown and I was part of many of the family activities. I am quite certain that I would not have done well as a servant in one of the great houses.

At your advice I shared my questions and concerns, which I have been too frightened to investigate, with Thomas. He is a very good listener. After taking a few notes, he advised me to keep questioning and thinking but to do nothing that would indicate that these issues are bothering me and to talk with no one else about them. This is not difficult. I confide in very few people and our typical British reserve keeps one from being asked personal questions. It is easy to remain private while interacting with others on a daily basis.

Before I left London, Thomas gave me an address at which I was to wire him if I notice anything different or suspicious. Two weeks ago I walked to the Steyning post office to send a wire informing him that Harriet was uncharacteristically away when I returned to Michelsgrove. His return wire, which he ordered held at the post office rather than delivered, recommended that I continue with my daily routine as though nothing had happened. So until she returned, I cared for the house as usual as well as cooking for Mr. Malthorpe, who seemed pensive but not terribly distressed. Each day I asked if Mrs. Malthorpe would be dining with us. That is all that I needed to know and, therefore, all that I asked.

I have wired Thomas twice since then; once when I made a discovery and then again when Harriet returned after having been away at least five days. While she was gone, I took the opportunity to give her room a thorough cleaning. I discovered that the chair that had become heavy was once again light and empty beneath the cushions. I then proceeded to her wardrobe to make certain that her clothing was not in ill repair. The only articles missing were her gabardine suit and one rather utilitarian summer dress.

Checking the two Harris Tweed suits that remained in the cupboard led me to a rather startling discovery. Each of the suits had been somewhat altered. Upon close inspection, I found that a series of uniquely formed compartments had been created in the wide seam allowances by removing some stitches and adding others. While carefully examining these compartments, I found only one object, a crumpled piece of extremely light weight silk on which was printed a map of Lisbon.

After each wire, I received a return message from Thomas containing only the words: "thank you." I now have two reasons to walk to Steyning six days a week.

Something else unsettles me. Perhaps it is my imagination or merely the stress of wartime but during our last two journeys to London, I have suspected that Wills and I were being followed. I have been wracking my brain to determine what facts led to that eerie feeling. The only person who I remember seeing on the train both times was a very nondescript woman. I took notice only because she reminded me of Miss Marple, a character from Agatha Christie's 1930 book, "Murder at the Vicarage."

I noticed this woman only because Wills had fallen asleep and I had foolishly not packed a book. To pass the time I found myself examining her coat and hat and, once she removed them, her suit, blouse, broach and handbag, trying to cast her in my mind pruning her roses, meeting with the dreaded Mrs. Price-Ridley, and finally solving the mystery. Though she did not look at me, she must have noticed my attention because she changed seats at the Hove station, moving to one of the compartments behind us.

I had thought that I glimpsed her again on our homeward bound train and also on our next trips to and from London. However, on these journeys I had remembered to bring a book.

So, dear cousin, am I on the verge of a big discovery; something dangerous? Or I am escaping the war by fantasizing that a popular fictional character is following me? Should I find myself encountering Hercule Poirot, one of Miss Christie's other sleuths, I shall know that I have begun the descent into madness.

What would I do without you, dear Margaret?

Please give my best regards to all and especially to Charles and the children.

Much love,
Moira

*****

July 31, 1942

My Dear Moira,

I am so pleased that the time you have spent with Thomas has been enjoyable and that he has relieved you of some of your fears. But now you think you are being followed?! Have you discussed this with Thomas?

Do you know where the mystery lady boards the train? The fact that she is a figure who has appeared four times during your trips to London, leads me to believe that she is not just a woman resembling a character in a book who happens to be traveling on the same train as you. That she frequently appears in the same place as you is too unusual for you not to

sit up and take note! Perhaps, should you see her again on the train, or anywhere for that matter, you should try to engage her in a conversation by letting her know that you have seen her before...you know... kindred travelers.

Your employer is a different kettle of fish, so to speak. From what I have read of Lisbon, it is a den of spies. Why would Harriet have a map of the same city and be missing for several days, unless she herself is a spy? Why does she leave her husband at home? It would seem that traveling as husband and wife would provide them a better cover, unless he is not a spy. If he is not involved, does he suspect her as you do?

You have your plate filled with mysteries!

I am so happy for Wills and for his lady friend. They both deserve to find happiness, considering all the grief in their lives. It's wonderful that they have found each other.

Our daily life in the U.S. has been changed somewhat in the past couple of months with the institution of more rationing. I mentioned the rationing of rubber in a previous letter, but now it also includes meat, coffee, gas, silk, nylon, and fuel oil. Individuals must demonstrate a need to purchase autos, tires, appliances and even typewriters.

Our block wardens check for compliance during blackouts. They make certain that windows have been covered and lights doused. Many people have painted the top half of their auto's headlights black.

On a happier note, I think that Gillian is quite pleased with her move, despite being much busier than she ever was in Chicago. Perhaps it's my imagination, but I think that part of the reason she moved was that she recognized that her leisure life was stagnant and that a change would be good. She has become very daring! Her weekends are just as full as her weekdays. She also volunteers at Baxter General Hospital, plays Bridge with a group she met through work, and enjoys going to the movies. She comes here often for dinner on Sundays, or she cooks for us.

William has benefited by her move. He mows, edges her garden beds, and weeds. He is learning which plants are weeds and which aren't. The first week he worked, he pulled up all of her newly planted lobelia before she could stop him. She now feels that she can leave him to do the work while she is not there, but at first, it took every ounce of patience she could muster to teach him what she wanted pulled!

Gillian's neighbor was so impressed by William's hard work that he hired him, too. The best part of all of this is that he can walk to his "job" and has a little money of his own in addition to his allowance.

He, of course, also does our lawn. However, when he works at home he has help. Bert crawls on his hands and knees to do the edging (nothing stops that child!). They do not get paid: all the children have chores to do as members of the family.

However, every once in a while, I take the two "gardeners" and Catherine to the Park Inn Restaurant for hamburgers, milkshakes, and French fries—all of which they adore.

The restaurant looks somewhat questionable as it is next to a tavern, with only a narrow alley separating the buildings. However, the place is clean and is popular with the doctors and nurses who work across the street at Sacred Heart Hospital. In fact, we had lunch one day with Sarah Feingold who was just coming from an interview at Sacred Heart Nursing School, which is also nearby.

I must digress a moment and tell you about Sarah. Continental Baking, a national company, has bought Mr. Feingold's bakery business. His health had declined and although Sarah could manage the business herself, she really had little interest in doing so. Her father negotiated an excellent price for the business, but did not sell all of his recipes. It could be that his sons may someday wish to reenter the baking business, or perhaps it is just that they wanted to retain some of the family's "secrets." It apparently didn't matter to Continental, which has its own best seller, called *Wonder Bread*, which is one of the first "sliced" breads made for American consumption. Recently, it has returned to unsliced loaves because of the steel shortage. The company also adds vitamins and minerals, which are necessary to fight certain diseases, to the recipe as part of a government-sponsored way of enriching white bread.

Sarah, too, has been volunteering with the Red Cross at Baxter General Hospital. She is hoping to be accepted into the Sacred Heart School of Nursing Program in the fall. It's a well-respected, three-year program, founded by the Sisters of Providence when they first came to Spokane in 1898.

The day we saw her she was very upbeat and said that she felt as if she had done well in her interview. She hopes to hear something positive by late August. We are keeping our fingers crossed!

Now back to the children. Bert has another job in addition to the yard work. This job pays something.

Six of my Service League friends have small children. The women often take turns watching each other's offspring during the summer months. Bert contracted with them to be a weekly storyteller for their collective group of 12.

Each week during the summer months, one of the mothers entertains all of the children at her home while the other women are grocery shopping or running whatever short errands they can do in two hours. Bert still "lives" at the public library and not only brings home books for himself, but also books to read to his young charges. They sit quietly for about twenty minutes, while Bert regales them with his stories. The ladies love him and so do the children. The host mother pays him almost as much as William's "clients" do!

Charles' unit was just activated. He does not know a deployment date. It is like a very bad dream! I don't even like to think about it as it upsets me so. Forgive me if I can't tell you anything other than that he is going somewhere, sometime. My next letter will undoubtedly be emotionally packed.

When last I wrote, we were going to the lake to open the cottage. Upon doing so, we discovered that yet again, someone had been inside. There was evidence of a fire in the fireplace, but the cottage was very neat and clean and nothing appeared amok. Nonetheless, it's frustrating to find that a person or persons unknown have entered your home. Yoshi could not come with us that particular weekend. I still cannot say with any certainty whether she did or did not alert Haruki if he, indeed, is the uninvited guest. In your last letter you had a wonderful suggestion regarding the cottage; that of renting it. We did, in fact, do just that! For the months of June and July we have leased the place. It is good that the boys are otherwise occupied, as all of the children were initially very upset. We will spend the entire month of August there, so they are happy at that prospect. The arrangement is fortuitous, now that we know that Charles will be leaving us soon. He will take as much time from the newspaper as he is allowed to be with us at the lake until he must deploy.

I am very lucky to have work that is so flexible as to have four weeks of vacation time. However, things are changing there as well. Several young doctors in Spokane have already been called into the armed services. Consequently, there will be a shortage of trained physicians. I may have to take on more hours. I am not happy with that situation as the children have more demands than Yoshi can fill.

Moira, I am so glad that you have a way to contact Thomas. I am praying for your safety.

With love,
Margaret

*****

September 9, 1942

My Dearest Margaret,

How thrilled I was to hear from you. Your letters are always a treat but this one was most anxiously anticipated. I have been very concerned for you as you cope with all the changes that war brings. I pray that all will go well for everyone.

William sounds like a very motivated entrepreneur, setting up a business for himself. That bodes well for his future. I can imagine that Gillian and her neighbor are both thrilled to have his help. With so many men gone to war and so many women taking jobs I predict that he will soon be forced to hire helpers or to turn down business.

As women enter war, those without mothers or mothers-in-law may need childcare as well. In our village, children help their parents at work or play with friends until their mothers' workdays are over. However, in London, hoards of children run the streets unsupervised.

Thomas and I have gone into an American cafeteria where I was able to taste a hamburger. Even though he complained that the patty was half as thick as it would be in Spokane, to me it was so very tasty and I was not hungry again for many hours. Thomas informed me that the 'fries' are what we English call 'chips' and that he thinks that those here are actually better than those at home.

Wonder Bread sounds very intriguing. Our ABC Tea Shops serve aerated bread, that is, bread with no yeast, only injected carbonic acid gas. Their shops are a bit less fancy than the Lyons Tea Shops where I often go during my time in London.

May I say how very proud I was that my suggestion to rent the cabin for part of the summer was helpful to you. After all that you have done to help me in every way I am gratified to be able to do something for you.

Although it should have come as no surprise, I was shocked that Charles has been called into active duty. I pray that his group will be spared the worst warfare. I imagine that your talent and training will soon be in heavy demand with so many male physicians being called into service.

Your concerns about Harriet are very well taken. I did share them with Thomas when I was last in London with Wills. Thomas' response was most disconcerting to me. I raised my findings in a casual conversation as we walked home from a delightful laugh-filled dinner on the first night of my last visit. His uncharacteristically serious reaction made me glad that we had enjoyed our meal before I told him. He has never spoken to me in such a tone and I took very careful notice. He insisted that we stop in one of the all night teashops for further conversation and steered me to a table in an isolated corner. He apparently did not notice that his change in demeanor had already brought me to full attention because immediately as he sat down with two cups of tea and said: "You must listen very carefully and follow my directions to the letter." He then gave me a list of 'orders' to follow.

First, he directed me to book two tickets for the day before Wills and I actually planned to return to Brackham Wood from London. Thomas later purchased two tickets for the next day and he and I exchanged them for those that I had purchased. I did not share this ticket swapping information with Wills, thinking that it would upset him. I think perhaps I should have.

Secondly, Thomas asked me to be very mindful of my traveling companions and particularly to look for 'Miss Marple' on the journey. If I did see her, I was to ignore her entirely and act as if I had no idea that she was aboard the train. He asked me to memorize a telephone number where I could leave a message for him at any time. He directed me to call when I arrived home and report whether or not I had seen her on the return train. This means of communication is faster and also more convenient for me than sending wires. I need only to walk to the nearest phone box.

Thomas' last directive was for me to gather together the things that I hold most dear into one place and to fit them into a bag that I could grab if I was directed to walk away from Michelsgrove, my home for the past seven years. I imagine that he thought that this last task would be difficult. It was not. After many years in service, my private possessions are very few. They include pictures of my parents, your letters, my postal savings book, scarves and one broach I kept from the three in my mother's jewelry case. I have no idea whether it was the most valuable but I loved it the most. It has a green central stone surrounded by petals of golden wire.

I was highly anxious on the journey back to Brackham Wood and had a very difficult time not reacting when, at the stop before ours, I recognized the woman. She was wearing a large hat that nearly hid her face. She was travelling with us after all. I then knew that the knowledge of our schedule must have been coming from the clinic where Wills was receiving his treatments. In retrospect, it seems obvious: of course, those at the clinic knew our schedule.

I assume that Thomas orchestrated the ticket exchange to determine where the information was coming from. Had someone been spying on me, they would have boarded the train a day earlier.

The world looks different to me since that journey. At first I found myself in an extreme state of alertness. My peripheral vision was widened and I became aware of every movement around me. My nerves felt as though they had migrated to every inch of my skin. Colours were brighter, my mind worked faster, my reflexes sped up, time slowed down and I had difficulty sleeping.

I could not long remain in such a state and eventually took a Sunday during which I sat and thought and did as little as possible. Gradually my nerves crept back under my skin and time has resumed its accustomed pace. However, I am changed.

I feel as though I am a newcomer here. One of the songs that I listen to on the wireless is an America tune written after the last war called: "How Ya Gonna Keep 'Em Down on the Farm?" Could that be what is happening to me as I became more and more comfortable in London? Perhaps it is the open way of communicating that you and I have developed, free of the fear of saying the wrong thing or expressing an opinion. When Thomas arrived, he and I began to communicate easily and freely from the beginning. Should I say something he does not agree with, he will tell me so or tease me and all is forgotten. I am proud that I am learning to gently tease back.

Of course when I return to the village, I must move back into the careful communication that will not earn me the silent treatment. That may not sound like such a bad thing but it is an extremely effective means of community control. Living in these small villages can be miserable when one is not looked at or spoken to on the streets, while standing in food lines, in the pub or even at church.

On a different note, Marie Hastings, whose husband, Jeb, was the foreman of the crew digging trenches in our park five years ago, has daughters aged 13 and 16 and is very concerned about the girls. When the war began Julia and Janet were 10 and 13 and not the least bit interested in the opposite sex. Now, with the severe shortage of single men, these GIs look very good to young single girls and widows. I dare say they also look good to a few of the women whose husbands are stationed in other parts of England or off fighting in North Africa.

I keep my position with the Malthorpes despite the fact that very few women now keep household help. Most housewives have been forced to go it alone in the struggle with meal planning and laundry. That, with the added rationing on sweets, chocolate and biscuits makes life quite grim for them. Growing gardens with root vegetables is now absolutely essential and more neighbors are also keeping a few chickens. Some who do not have chickens themselves exchange their leftover scraps for an egg each week with those who do.

Harriet Malthorpe arrived home the day after I returned from London. The silence and tension in the house is now nearly unbearable. Never a word is exchanged between her and George. It is as though he is being shunned. Only absolutely essential words pass between Harriet and me. However, when I see George on the pavement, he is most pleasant.

This constant anger and tension is very hard to deal with and, therefore, I rarely stay in the house while Mrs. M. is there, which is, by the way, many more hours than before. Your comment that Lisbon is a hotbed of spies got my attention. During wartime only the military, the press, and spies are able to travel easily. Harriet now checks frequently for the mail delivery, seems distracted and insists on answering the door herself. It is as though she is waiting for something. I cannot imagine what. Perhaps it is a message.

As I prepare for the London trip this coming weekend, I shall pack my few treasures in the bottom of my Gladstone bag—just in case. I have a penchant for visiting Malcolm but shall discuss it with Thomas before I act.

About Thomas—I have no one else in whom to confide my thoughts and feelings so it must be you, dear cousin. Should you not wish to respond, I will understand perfectly.

Thomas and I have such a natural relationship, laughing, talking and peeking about London. He seems so familiar, as though I have known him all of my life. I find myself wanting to discuss my impressions of life with him at the end of every day. I am sure that he is charming, jolly and helpful to everyone.

If this letter sounds like I am at sixes and sevens, it is because I am. I shall take it to the post box before it becomes even more so.

Please know that my thoughts and prayers are with you all, including Gillian.

Love,
Moira

*****

October 10, 1942

My Dearest Moira,

One thing I know for certain...I'm so glad that you did not follow my advice regarding the stranger on the train. Confronting her would have been a very big mistake in light of what you now know. Thomas is certainly much more knowledgeable about how to handle situations such as yours. He obviously knows more about or suspects something more untoward and unpleasant about your employer than you and I have even considered.

It sounds as if home life for the Malthorpes isn't very pleasant either. I shudder to think of you in the middle of something of which you know so little. By that I mean, so little about what Harriet is really doing. I suppose if it's a matter of King and country,

England is fortunate to have you in this mess. Nonetheless it is a great worry to us.

Your marching orders are so specific; it would seem that Thomas views life in Brackham Wood as very serious and perhaps even temporary for you; I'm glad that he has provided for your quick evacuation, if need be.

It makes me smile to think of the two of you strolling the streets of London or sipping tea in a midnight tea shop. You eating hamburgers and fries?! Why, you are becoming Americanized, my dear cousin!!! By the way, I doubt that Thomas is "charming, jolly, and helpful with *everyone*." It's more likely that he responds that way to someone he cares about in a special way.

About two weeks after we had arrived home from our month at the lake, we received a phone call from the farmer at the south end of Newman Lake who occasionally drops by to check on our cottage. His name is Ben Silver.

Ben and his wife Marion have four children, the eldest of whom is a 16-year-old son, whose given name I don't know, but everyone calls him Chip.

Chip is allowed to drive the truck on country roads only. He had been sent by his father to check on a neighbor's cottage, which is near ours. The road on the west side of the lake is very windy and as Chip was rounding one of the curves, he lost control of the truck and it rolled down an embankment. Chip was trapped inside.

Most of the summer people had returned to town for the season. However, one person, who coincidentally was none other than Haruki, heard the sound of the crash!

Haruki had been camping in the woods behind our cottage the entire summer. I suppose he was getting set to move into the cottage again, knowing that we were not to return. I say "knowing" because he has been in contact with Yoshi from the time that the strange letters began to arrive in our mailbox in town.

Initially, Haruki was in Canada, just across the Washington border. Then he came to Spokane and lived in some flophouse downtown while he and Yoshi came up with a plan to keep him hidden. Yoshi has kept him apprised for months of our scheduled use of the cottage to include that of our renters.

She has also kept him supplied with blankets, clothes, and money. He, in turn, has become somewhat of a recluse, living in the woods, when he did not have access to the cottage and hiding inside when he knew we would not be there.

But I digress, yet again. Upon hearing the crash, Haruki set out to find the source of the noise and discovered Chip pinned in the truck. He managed to get the boy out and learned where he lived. Haruki covered him with one of his blankets and left Chip on the ground beside the truck. He then ran to the farm and brought Ben back to the site.

The short version of the story is that Chip is recovering nicely and the Silvers, ever grateful to Haruki, have found work for him on their farm, as well as a cozy spot in which to live. Haruki now enjoys the warmth and security of a very small, unused bunkhouse on their property.

I find the seeming lack of racial bias on the part of the Silvers to be amazing and commendable! The family is very religious which may account in some small part for their acceptance of Haruki. Whatever the reason, Yoshi and we are grateful for their kindness.

Yoshi has acknowledged her complicity in all of this drama. She wanted to leave as she felt disgraced, but for the time being she is still with us.

I am hoping that she will stay as I need her now more than ever.

My darling Charles is due to depart for training in a couple of days. His unit was ordered into active military service in mid-September. The unit will be reorganized at an undisclosed location in Oregon. There they will begin training with other activated units as a Division in preparation for deployment to Europe. We know not the date they will leave. At least for the time being, Charles will not be in the thick of war.

It seems that all our men are going somewhere; a steady stream of loved ones leaving our city, while an even longer line of military men and their families take their place. It's terrifying and at the same time the feeling of patriotic duty outweighs everything. American flags are displayed everywhere.

A while ago, we got the scare of our lives. A Japanese incendiary bomb was dropped in a forest in eastern Oregon in an attempt to ignite a forest fire. An airplane, carrying the bomb, had been catapulted from a submarine off the coast.

Fortunately, a forest ranger heard the sound of the plane and spotted the smoke. He reported the fire and by the time authorities reached the site, it was just smoldering, leaving only a crater and remnants of the bomb. The military confirmed it as a Japanese bomb, as there were identifying markings on the nose cone. They attempted to keep the information secret but the newspapers learned of the incident and soon the word was spread from the West Coast to the East Coast. The Blue Mountains, where the drop took place, is about 200 miles from Spokane—too close if you ask me!

Please, Moira, stay alert and do not think twice about contacting Thomas if anything, ANYTHING, does not feel right! Yes, you must move back into careful communication with your neighbors as that will keep you from being shunned, but above all else you must keep yourself safe!

With love and concern,
Margaret

*****

November 15, 1942

My Dearest Margaret,

As always, I was elated upon receipt of your letter. It is hard to believe how much our lives have changed since we first wrote over five years ago.

The Tsutakawa family certainly has brave members in the persons of Haruki and Yoshi. I had wondered whether and, perhaps secretly hoped, that your squatter was Haruki rather than some miscreant with bad intentions. I remember reading that Yoshi was particularly tense once when you had visited your property with little notice.

I hold such stories to my heart whenever I feel discouraged about man's inhumanity to man. It helps me fight away the despair that always looms in the back of my mind. Just when we began to relax in the certainty that Hitler had all of his weapons pointed in other directions, incidents such as the bombings last April through June of Exeter, Bath, York, Norwich, and Canterbury shake us from our complacency. They have come to be referred to as the Baedeker Bombings, as Hitler chose them because they are featured cathedral cities with three-star ratings in the Baedeker Tourist Guides.

We have now become inured to the sound of the RAF flying overhead at night and the U.S. Army Air Corps flying overhead during the daytime on their flights to and from North Africa and Germany.

I know that you will miss Charles terribly and am grateful that you have a support system and worthy work that will help you get through the time he is gone. Even though there is no certainty, his posting in Oregon sounds better than some and is certainly closer to home than England, the Pacific, Morocco or Algeria. I will keep you all in my prayers and thoughts.

Today is a marvelous day. Church bells all over the country are ringing again for the first time since they were silenced after Dunkirk early in June of 1940, not to be rung except as a warning of a German invasion. On this past Thursday, November 11, British troops under the leadership of Field Marshall Montgomery defeated the troops of General Rommel at El Alamein. The BBC announced in advance that the bells would begin ringing again today lest anyone fear invasion.

How hard it is to describe the feelings raised by such sounds. You may remember how the bells sounded four times each hour during daylight hours. When they stopped two years ago the silence thundered.

I am writing you from London where I have been for the greater part of a week. Yesterday a chance encounter caused me to understand what a sheltered life I have lived. Since the sun was shining I chose to ride to Wills' clinic on the open top of a double-decker bus rather than in the tube. The ride is slower but much more pleasant than being underground on a beautiful day. The particularly well-cut suit on the woman sitting opposite caught my attention.

The woman returned my gaze and I was abashed, lest I had been staring. She then asked if I was Miss Edwards. I was shocked. English strangers do not break the silence between them unless it is perfectly obvious that the person to whom they are speaking comes from a lower social order, for example, a hotel doorman. Short of a dire emergency, no one would risk speaking first to someone of a higher class.

Americans have no such reservations and I am becoming accustomed to Tom readily bursting into conversation with people on the street. At first, I felt embarrassed each time. However, I soon learned that the moment a person heard his gentle American accent and experienced his beautiful smile, they spoke to him easily.

Now back to the woman in the tweed suit. I replied that I was, indeed, Miss Edwards and she revealed that she was Emily Mayview, the eldest of the four Mayview children. It is with her family that I was placed when my parents died. I will always be grateful to them for their care and consideration for three years until I recovered from the shock of losing my parents and leaving school.

I had always remembered her as much younger than myself but, in reality, she is only five years my junior. The difference between ages 9 and 14 is much greater than those between 33 and 38. I was gratified to learn that the family has always spoken of me with affection and fondly remembered my years with them. Emily and

I exchanged contact information and I look forward to visiting with her when I am next in London.

Happy as I am to have seen Emily, our visit made me aware of the fact that, like a child, I have never lived in a home of my own. I have not so much as lived in a bedsitter within someone else's home. I have never let a flat, fed a gas meter, or signed a rental agreement. I am as a child. I am once again at sixes and sevens.

I will soon need to leave my work with the Malthorpe family. No other household in Brackham Wood still employs a housemaid and it is very difficult to keep up the pretense of a normal situation. There is also the strong possibility that I may need to pick up my bag of belongings and disappear from view at any time. I feel like I am standing on the edge of a precipice waiting for the signal to jump.

With men leaving to fight in the war, women are taking up jobs as factory workers, bus conductors, some even work in banks. Like me, some of these women have been in service all of their lives and yet they manage to survive far away from the homes they have known.

I have neither the credentials to become a typewriter, which is a person who operates a typewriting machine, nor a certificate to become a teacher. I do not even have experience as a waitress. Therefore, the funds you send me each month are my only source of peace. I am so grateful. With that sum of money, and the small amount I saved up for my imagined bookshop, I believe I can survive for more than a few months if necessary. And, of course, there is also the amount from your legacy, which I have put by for the sole purpose of traveling to you.

I am inspired by stories of other women who have jumped from one life to another. For instance, your cousin Gillian, who lived with Aunt Elizabeth and Uncle Basil until she was over 35, after which she took over their home, converted it to a boarding house, took a job in factory security and then moved 2,000 miles to take a similar position in a new company. She even purchased her own home; something which very few women in this country are able to do.

When I get the signal from Thomas to make my move, I shall no doubt have to disappear into the city. It would be impossible to vanish into a country village. Since my last letter to you, I have travelled twice to London as Wills' companion and each time my same friend, tracker, or stalker was on the same train, albeit not in the same carriage in which I was travelling. Is Harriet or George or Robert Gentry or Malcolm or "Miss Marple" watching me? What is it that they think I know?

Your assurance has given me courage to relax and enjoy his company. We talk for hours, enjoy eating out together, visit such museums and public buildings as are still open and take in theater and concerts. We also walk frequently in the parks, and enjoy other pleasures together.

Please give my love to all in the family. Cherish every minute.

All my love,
Moira

*****

December 29, 1942

My Dearest Cousin Moira,

I apologize for not getting this letter posted sooner. I had so wanted to send you glad tidings and

have my wishes arrive by the holiday, but time just got away from me. A belated Merry Christmas! I hope you like the enclosed hankie; it was one of my mother's.

Charles was able to get brief leave in early December; that was the first of our *two* Christmases. While Charles was here, he and I pretended that he was home for good, knowing full well that was not the case. The children were so happy to see their father; the boys especially, as they loved to hear his "training" stories. Catherine was glad that her Papa was home, but the lure of Santa coming in a couple of weeks was just as strong as having her father here. The boys played along with Santa's midnight visit on the 24th and then tried to be brave when the reality of not having Charles here set in.

Whenever a letter from you arrives, I am relieved; I read it and then I am worried all over again! Your world is upside-down, but I'm so glad to know that you are still safe. Were I not to hear from you, now that Charles can no longer contact Thomas through the paper, I do not know what I would do. I suppose I would have to camp at the entrance of the paper until they contacted Thomas for me!

Yoshi is still with us, but the sadness and guilt she feels are still so overwhelming that she has become more of a patient than a nanny. I am reluctant to let her go, as I cannot imagine where she would go. I wonder, however, whether she might heal more quickly, or at the very least not be reminded daily of the shame she perceives, were she to leave.

It is amazing that, although she is American-born Japanese, her soul responds as would those of her ancestors. I am trying to find her work outside our home during the hours the children are in school. She is a very good housekeeper and always has all her tasks completed with time leftover. The remaining time is the problem for that is when the thoughts of deceptions past come creeping in again. The Pay'n Takit Store where we shop is within walking distance of our house. The manager knows Yoshi as our housekeeper. I inquired as to hourly jobs and was told that she could be hired as a grocery bagger. If I can convince her that a job away from our house for a few hours a week is a good thing, perhaps it will calm her anxiety. I must add that it bothers me that a college graduate can only find work as a grocery bagger. I am well aware that being Japanese is the reason.

The ringing of the bells and the roar of the RAF and the U.S. Army Air Corps planes above you, though acoustically opposite, must be somewhat comforting. At least you know that either a victory has occurred or that the fighters are in the air to protect the citizenry! We read about Montgomery's success!

I can certainly understand why you feel so anxious at this time of your life. The uncertainty alone would contribute enough anxiety to drive one mad. You on the other hand are not just anyone. You are a brave, courageous woman who when forced into this situation has responded with pluck and nerve. I dare say that your fears of doing something you have never done, as you may have to do should Thomas alert you to move, will all but disappear once you have left Brackham Wood.

Imagine yourself in 1937, when we first began our correspondence. I wonder whether you would recognize yourself today as that same woman. Five years ago, you couldn't drive a vehicle, you didn't have a bank account, and you did not dare to raise your eyes from the pavement lest they meet those of your neighbors, or heaven forbid someone not of your "class." To feed a meter or let a flat you may never have done, but were you to be faced with either, you undoubtedly would succeed with flying colors! Do not be deterred or afraid, my dear Moira! I'm so glad that you met Emily Mayview; perhaps she could help you, if need be, with any of the details of resettling.

In the U.S., women are faced with challenges similar to yours. The difference is that we support one another and despite "class" barriers, which do exist here, women are women first. "Class consciousness" by a few affects only a small population of women.

I have struggled for the last few months wanting to do something in the service of my country. Obviously, I cannot leave my children. Even if I could, as a woman, I would not be accepted into any of the Services, yet, that is.

In 1941, Emily Dunning Barringer was elected president of the American Medical Women's Association. She is awe-inspiring! In 1902, she became the first woman resident and ambulance physician of New York City's Gouverneur Hospital. She is in the news again—40 years later. She is now fighting for women's right to hold appointments in the Army and Navy Medical Corps. It's too late for me but I can't wait for what she and others will undoubtedly achieve in the future.

I have resigned from the Women and Children's Clinic and have taken a contract position at Baxter General Hospital. This is the hospital of which I spoke of in an earlier letter. The facility has recently been completed. Although we are told it is temporary, the 1,500 bed-hospital looks anything but that. It is laid out with single-story wood buildings that have pitched roofs, which look just like barracks. The 150 buildings sprawl over the 220 plus acres in the northern part of Spokane. I'm going to need roller-skates to get from one department to another!

I begin work in a couple of days. My pay is less and I must work a five-day week but I will be involved in getting our injured troops healthy again and I hope this fills the need I feel to be involved.

Convalescent care has changed dramatically. No longer are patients kept in bed until considered ambulatory. With new methods, those soldiers returning to duty are going to be in better shape, both physically and mentally than when they initially deployed. I will be involved with diagnosing each patient's condition and then prescribing a treatment. My earlier work in the Clinic with depressed women, in which I prescribed a regimen of physical activities, was one of the reasons that I think I was hired. The regimen can be easily adapted to fit a male profile. In addition to physical therapy, occupational therapy has become absolutely necessary in helping the patients relearn skills and discover new ones.

Red Cross volunteers provide the patients with recreational activities and entertainment. I'm hoping to see Sarah, if she still has time to volunteer; perhaps not, as she was accepted to nurses' training.

I do not want to embarrass you, but I must ask this question. You are fast becoming accustomed to the brashness and forwardness of Americans, so considering that I am your cousin in addition to being one of those very open Americans, what did you *really* mean when you said that you and Thomas were "enjoying walks in the park and *other pleasures*"? Hooray for you if you have found love in the midst of terror. I couldn't be happier for you and Thomas. The only thing I will add is the following: I hope you are taking precautions.

   With love and pride in you,
   Margaret

*****

January 20, 1943

My Dearest Margaret,

   Thank you so much for your gift and your most encouraging and supportive letter. No gift could be better than a handkerchief that once belonged to your mother—my most beloved Aunt Elizabeth. I had often regretted not saving one from my own mother and I now I can forgive myself.

   I am proud to hear that you have gone to work at Baxter Hospital. The need is great and your children are old enough to allow you to manage the household and have special time with them as well. Do you travel by train, bus, or automobile to reach the hospital from your home?

   I wonder if you could talk to Yoshi and make her see how important it is to the war effort that she stay with your family and allow you to do this important and patriotic medical work. She is part of your family by now and, with hers being interned, she needs you as much as you need her. I am sure that her shame is burned deep within her by her cultural upbringing but perhaps if she can think of her work with you as her patriotic duty, her pain will be lessened.

Your responses to my last letter helped me see where I was in my life and gave me courage to look at things in a new way. Your faith in me gave me the motivation that I needed to move on. Particularly comforting was your assurance that, once I let go of Brackham Wood, my fears would vanish.

Wills has progressed to the point where he can move around with his two sticks and is able to take care of most of his own needs. Last month he came to a turning point. We began to meet here in Brackham Wood almost daily for a cup of tea and a good talk. These daily chats became very important to him and we began to make them a priority. I realized that he had no one to talk with as I have you. He had no one to whom he could unburden himself of his deepest fears and feelings. His mind and spirit seemed to return to him quickly once we began this exchange.

He had been very depressed, not merely because of the pain and burdens of his injury, but because he can no longer contribute toward the war effort. This was not because of peer pressure but because he had felt he had nothing to contribute. I was so thrilled when he began sounding a bit like his old self and he was happy to discover that once he began to talk freely his mind became clearer and began to work faster.

When I heard him say something indicating an interest in or curiosity about something I began to encourage him in that direction. I also did something that you have done for me over these five years. When I heard him put forward a list of objections to making a change, I carefully began to help him examine those obstacles to see if they were truly impediments.

Unconsciously I was nudging him as you have been nudging me.

Wills and my friendship has grown to the point it had reached before the war. I rejoice in seeing the spark in him once again. He expressed a desire to begin attending church and I assist him in getting there. You may remember that, in the pre-war years, Wills and I both attended church at St. Peter's in Brackham Wood on Sunday but pretended that we were strangers during the service. We then met afterwards to spend Sunday afternoons together. This time round we sit together during the service and also afterward for a cup of tea and conversation.

Vicar Dimblebey had begun an after church 'tea and conversation' in the church hall during the Battle of Britain. When the rationing of tea began, he asked anyone who had an extra tea coupon to bring it to him so that he could keep the event going. So important had the after-church-tea become that, despite our shortages, he never needed to ask again. Occasionally someone brings a cake or biscuits to share. Even if it needs to be cut into the smallest of pieces, sharing a sweet brings us much joy.

After reading and rereading your last letter several times, I became aware that even though I was frightened and lacked confidence, I had already made up my mind to move on from Brackham Wood, although I could not imagine how that would occur. The answer came to me when Wills revealed that June Beattie, who had been his nurse in London, had written that she had found a temporary part-time placement for him in London. Before the war he had been in demand all over the county because of his skill with horses and a new program has begun whereby work was being sought for handicapped soldiers who could not return to the battlefield.

A position was created for him in which he will advise the young boys who are now taking care of the royal horses. I imagine that Nurse Beattie was instrumental in creating this position. She is quite interested in keeping Wills in London, particularly since his optimism has returned. He will never be the same physically but he can manage to move around with the help of his sticks. What a gift.

My dear Margaret, please make certain that you are seated as I tell what I have done.

While I was very happy for Wills, I was then faced with the prospect of returning to the Malthorpes without the frequent trips to London. I realized that I can no longer do that and, with your encouragement and that of Thomas, I packed up my core belongings and seasonal clothing just as though I was taking Wills there for his regular visit, even though I did not plan to return.

I failed to mention that "Miss Marple" was no longer riding our trains but had been replaced with a rather nondescript man, noticeable only because he is on the youngish side for a man not in uniform, perhaps 40 to 45. After I took Wills to the clinic for the last time, Thomas met me. He quickly became aware that we were both being followed. With Thomas toting my bag and frequent turns, it took only minutes to get away.

So what has happened since I relocated in London? Except for Thomas, I am alone with no contacts and no idea of how to find work. I am currently living again in Mary Anne's house but do not know how long she will have a room available. She has mentioned that one of her schoolmates was coming to London and I wonder if that is perhaps a hint that the room I have been living in will soon become unavailable to me.

Thomas and I celebrated the arrival of 1943 together in London. It seemed as though everyone poured out onto the streets on that cloudless night. The waning moon provided just enough illumination to tempt masses of people to venture outside. As usual, the city was blacked out to prevent it from becoming a target for German bombers. However, we joked that the noise alone may attract them.

I found a very old but lovely black dress decorated with jet beads in one of the 'make do and mend' shops. It looked as though a dowager duchess had worn it many years past. I altered it to fit and had my hair cropped in quite a fashionable style. We began the evening at a party and, much to my shock and surprise, both Robert Gentry and Malcolm Blake were in the room. Neither of them recognized me. Thomas enjoyed introducing me first to Robert and then later to Malcolm. Robert looked, squinted and had a hard time believing it was me. Malcolm, however, was in complete denial. He argued with Thomas, saying that he had known Moira Edwards for over seven years and this certainly was not she. It wasn't until I burst out laughing that he realized that I was one and the same person. It has been said that nobody ever notices a servant. Perhaps that is true.

So here I am, living outside of Sussex for the first time in my life—no home, no means of support, not knowing what tomorrow will bring and, rather than being paralyzed with fear I feel a freedom that I have never before felt. I know I have taken the right step. I also know that I still have family support behind me, albeit 5,000 miles away.

***

Continued on February 16, 1943
***

As you may imagine, events have occurred at a frightening pace since I began this letter less than a month ago and I have not had a moment to reflect. I must, therefore, abbreviate all that has occurred and send it on the way to you. You will soon read the news that prompts me to get this letter into the post immediately.

On Thursday, January 28, I found work. The following weekend, I moved to a flat on Devonshire Street, near Regent's Park, thus the change of address on this letter. My work, though I am not at liberty to describe it fully, requires me to use many of the skills that I would have needed had I fulfilled my dream of working in my bookstore. The prospect of such work was daunting, but once I realized how well it suited me I began to enjoy it. The days, which sometimes run to ten or twelve hours long, seem to fly by.

But that, my dearest cousin, is not the big news. Two days ago on St. Valentine's Day, Thomas surprised me with a proposal I could not refuse. I signed a paper and yesterday afternoon found us at the registry office reciting our vows. How could the paperwork be done so fast? Thomas must have influence. He made me promise to write and post this letter to you before today is over. He wanted you to be the first to know, so that you can tell Charles.

I do thank you for your carefully worded advice at the end of your last letter. A woman who enjoys certain pleasures before time is referred to in England as "no better than she should be."

Our news will no doubt shock you but we feel so comfortable. I know this is right. Thomas asked me to assure you that he also is certain. Just now he is en route to 'our' Devonshire Street flat with his belongings.

So, for the moment, life is looking up. No bombs are falling, survivors of the German Sixth Army surrendered to Russia on January 30 and February 2, and I have become your sister-in-law as well as your cousin. Would that life always feel like this.

Please take care and give our love to my brother-in-law Charles and my beloved nephews and niece.

Much love,

Your cousin and sister,

Moira

*****

March 9, 1943

My Dearest sister Moira,

It gives me chills to call you 'sister.' I am overwhelmed with joy every time I think about your marriage to Thomas. Both Charles and I can scarcely believe that Thomas has chosen the woman, dearest to me, to be his wife! It's just unbelievable! Please tell Thomas that he is a scamp for keeping the secret, but that we love him dearly and wish both of you the very best.

What wonderful news about Wills. It seems that both you and he have found happiness and a way to serve your country at the same time. Please give him my regards and best wishes.

The War Effort is citywide in Spokane. Thousands have volunteered for various agencies. Spokane has been divided into nine districts. Each district has a block captain who checks houses for lights that may be showing during blackouts. Air Raid drills occur with alarming frequency. An air raid siren was installed on a nearby school, which, when there is a drill, jolts us from our beds or from whatever we might be doing at the time. It is quite frightening. The windows of the newspaper office have been covered by heavy black drapes and the skylights of the lovely Davenport hotel have been covered with black tar.

Because of lack of manpower and because some things have been used increasingly by the military, there are shortages. Rationing continues; most recently metal and bread have been rationed.

In fact, there was a full-page ad in the paper addressed to all citizens, particularly farmers, to check their property again for any scrap metal. We have been directed to work in groups to get the metal to the volunteer sites where it can then be sold and shipped to steel mills. The mills then use it for the production of war materiel.

I am very busy at work. Thank goodness Yoshi (she did take a job at the grocery store and seems to be doing better) is still with us. Some evenings I can barely move, let alone prepare a meal. The hospital area is so large that half of my time is spent getting from one clinic to another. I think that the distance from one area to another within the hospital is what accounts for my weariness. I find it very stimulating to be with physicians who have such excellent credentials and education. On the other hand, the maimed troops we see are in most cases heart-breaking. It is an understatement to say that war is horrid. What war has done to these brave young men is such a travesty.

At the very least, the grounds of the hospital are soothing and private. Four miles of pines, with walking paths will give the patients a place to be wheeled out-of-doors, or if they are ambulatory, to walk on pleasant days.

We have not been to the cottage since late October, but I plan to rent it as I did last summer. Gillian and I will take the children there for the month of August; that is if I can get that much time off from work. Otherwise, Gillian, who has time, will be there with them and I will come when I can. Haruki now keeps an eye on the place; it's a strange position for him after his months of camping out there without permission.

Gillian, too, is very involved in her job and works long hours. She now supervises security for close to 300 women employees at Brown Industries. There are a few men but the women seem to be just as capable as the men at their jobs. The company manufactures aluminum engine bearings and other parts for B-17s. Kaiser, which is located nearby provides the aluminum. Gillian's life is very full, but at the same time she is lonely. Her schedule is not conducive to finding romance.

The children have occupied themselves with school and projects on the weekends. William has found several snow shoveling jobs in our neighborhood, which add to his bank account; while Bert has continued his reading soirees on Saturday mornings. Catherine is a "Junior Girl Scout."

Her troop meets once a week, after school. They do craft pieces; learn first aid and childcare skills, and the like. Because of the sugar and butter shortage, a patriotic calendar sale has replaced their annual cookie sale as a community project. The girls also gather clothing for war victims.

Today is William's fifteenth birthday. He has become a man before my very eyes. I suppose it is in the absence of Charles that he feels he must leave his childhood behind. He is still not so grown-up that he has refused to celebrate his birthday. We very seldom have sweets, but on birthdays, how can we not? William has invited a couple of his classmates to be here. I love hearing the boys laughing and enjoying themselves; there are so many just a few years older than these boys who find themselves in the mud trenches of war.

I am thrilled to pieces at the very real prospect of actually seeing you. Our dreams of being together could be a reality. Stay safe, my dear. I know you cannot talk about your work, but whatever it is, do be careful. Can you tell me anything that will resolve the mystery of the Malthorpes?

With love,
Your sister Margaret

*****

June 15, 1943

My Dearest Margaret,

I am amazed that William is now fifteen years old. I pray that this war ends before he can even consider joining up. There are some hopeful signs that Germany is beginning to falter in its quest to rule all of Europe. The Japanese have also faced defeat. The victories of Midway and the Coral Sea last June and Guadalcanal more recently give me a glimmer of hope that the war will be soon ended.

I am glad to hear that you are able to practice medicine and grow in your profession while using your talents to help with the war effort. Many people, myself included, depend upon you so I am grateful that you take care of yourself. I am sad to hear that your life in America echoes ours. It is very difficult not to let rationing, blackouts, life changes, and isolation get us down during this long, long war.

Last week we traveled to Brackham Wood to pick up my warm weather clothing as well as a few small things I had left behind. Thomas very much wanted to see the places where I had lived and, while I looked forward to the visit, I felt a bit uncomfortable about how the town would greet me after my abrupt departure. Small villages can be unforgiving to those who have left.

I need not have worried. We travelled on a beautiful cloudless Saturday; each carrying a partially empty Gladstone bag to which we planned to add my belongings for the return journey. Brackham Wood looked beautiful as we pulled in on that sunny day. Bright green leaves vibrated with energy.

The minute we arrived, Tom suggested that we visit Vicar Dimblebey and his wife, Patricia. I protested that it might possibly be an inconvenience. He insisted, saying that after all he had heard about the couple, he was most anxious to meet them. As we began to walk up the hill toward the vicarage, my fears of being shunned vanished instantly. Henry Grimes and his chum ran across the street and nearly knocked us over in their eagerness to grab our bags. Henry was the cockney boy who had come to town four years ago when he and his sister Lucy were evacuated from London. Their parents were never found so both children changed their surnames to Johnson by deed poll and appear to be thriving.

The sunshine seemed to have coaxed every villager out onto the pavement. They passed us in the street with a nod and a hello, greeting me but looking mostly at Thomas. I admit to being proud as I walked beside such a handsome and healthy-looking man. In fact, I felt rather like a lady coming down from the manor for a walkabout. I was elated by the sunshine, the welcome, and especially by having Thomas by my side. How difficult it was to realize that this was the same street on which I once felt invisible.

I was shocked at the speed with which the Dimblebeys opened the door after we knocked. The boys put our luggage in the entry hall and departed after refusing the coins Thomas offered them. Patricia and the Vicar wore broad smiles as they ushered us into the parlor. Much to my surprise, my London landlady, Mary Anne Withers, and her sister, Phoebe Miles, were standing just inside the door. However, Thomas did not seem a bit surprised.

We were invited to lunch and chatted pleasantly. Over lunch, I was given the most wonderful surprise. St. Peter's Church was to host a reading of our vows the following morning. I blurted out my first thought, which was: "But I brought nothing to wear." After smiles all round the table, I was told that Phoebe, after telling George Malthorpe of the plan, had asked if she could look through my closet and choose something suitable for the occasion. She had chosen my Windsor blue spring frock, tacked on a capelet and cuffs of fine lace and fashioned a small hat from some of that same material, which came from a bolt of lace that had appeared on the sharing shelf of the church in December. Knowing that fabric was very hard to come by, Patricia Dimblebey had set it aside for the use of future brides.

I remembered that you had once written that I would look good in that color blue.

On Sunday morning, Thomas and I marched into the church behind the vicar during the processional. We sat in honored seats in the front pew and, rather than reading a full sermon, the vicar read a brief homily, after which we recited our vows in front of the congregation.

A special tea followed during which tiny slices of a traditional wedding fruitcake were served. I was very touched because I knew that the parishioners had donated precious ration coupons for the ingredients. Our picture was taken as we stood behind the cake. However, the cake itself was hidden underneath a cardboard cover decorated with icing. Many communities have created such cake covers because sugar is so precious. This cover had been used in five wedding receptions before ours.

The women praised Thomas to the hilt for being so thoughtful as to come up with such a lovely idea. I know that he is truly a wonderful man but I also know in my heart that he had some excellent guidance in planning and executing such a delightful celebration. In fact, I am so certain of that fact that I send you my profound gratitude. I had been perfectly happy with our registry office marriage but, as we returned to London, I realized why couples take part in public and religious ceremonies. They provide a lovely memory and a special feeling to carry throughout ones' life. Thank you.

I have recently left my first position after being transferred. I now work for the Home Office, the government ministry that includes police, and security service among other agencies. I was amazed to discover the present Home Secretary is a man by the name of Herbert Morrison for whom the Morrison shelter, which provided me a refuge during bombing raids, was named. Incidentally, he had taken over the position in 1940 from Sir John Anderson for whom the Anderson shelter was named.

In this position, I was originally stationed in reception, during which I daily directed hoards of people to their destinations. In doing so, questions that I had been mulling over in my mind were reactivated. First of al, I glimpsed Robert Gentry as he strode toward one of the lifts with great purpose. I had long suspected that Robert worked at something other than facilitating the moving of goods around the country as he had told me at the time. However, I was completely surprised on a later day when Malcolm Blake came striding through the lobby.

Being introduced to both Robert and Malcolm on New Years' Eve had caused me no suspicion. I had recently come from a small village where seeing an acquaintance in a new place was nothing exceptional. I now know that the chance of coming across a familiar face in a city of over four million inhabitants is very rare indeed. Thomas knew them from his work as a reporter. Were you to ask me in what line of work they met, I could confidently answer that they are in the information business.

During our visit to Brackham Wood, I learned that Harriet is now in the village only twice a month for about three days each time. Phoebe promised to be alert as to her comings and goings. You and I have long suspected that Harriet is in some type of secret work. Indications were: her signals on the downs, her frequent bicycle trips to the coast, her less than congenial relationship with her husband, George, her suits with extra fabric, her spike of happiness at the time of the feared German invasion, the books secreted in her chair and her untoward hysteria at an impending visit from her finishing school teacher, Monica Graves, who met her death soon thereafter.

I still have many questions about George. He and Harriet always made the regular visits to Aunt Jewell. Eventually I had begun to suspect that they were both information agents of some type.

Now that I work in the Home Office, some new words have been added to my vocabulary. One of them is "handler." A handler meets individually with a handful of secret agents who do not know one another. In these meetings, he collects the results of their last assignment and presents them with their next. The handlers then meet together to share and compare information.

So now I wonder whether or not George is also an agent or whether he merely travelled with Harriet to her meetings and then went about other business, such as visiting with Malcolm, his former co-worker and friend, while Harriet met her handler.

The longer my mind works on these connections, the more confused I become. Before the expected German invasion, anyone with a German background was suspected of being an enemy agent. Once the threat of invasion was lessened, perhaps there were concerns about weather reports or information on the location of strategic resources and factories being passed to the enemy.

So, if indeed, Harriet is working for the other side, what could she be watching now that the bombing raids are in abeyance and the German invasion force has turned toward Russia where it is suffering defeat after defeat?

I can only assume that the Germans are already aware that over one million Canadian and American soldiers have poured into England. We natives joke that it is only the barrage balloons that keep our island from sinking for all the North American soldiers that have 'invaded' our shores. And one final question: why were Wills and I being followed?

Dear Margaret, I constantly think of you and your family. Please give Catherine my belated birthday wishes and my love to Bert and William as well as Charles when you are able to contact him.

Love,

Sister and Auntie Moira

*****

August 2, 1943

My Dearest Moira,

You give me more credit than I deserve. Indeed, I did contact Thomas; a comical event in itself, which I shall endeavor to explain in a moment. I just want you to know that the surprise you found in the village was totally your husband's doing. I merely gave him a push and some names; the rest he managed on his own and from the description in your letter it sounds as if he was successful.

When you told me of your marriage and sudden move from Brackham Wood, I realized that you probably left in such a hurry that you had little or no time to explain what you were doing or where you were going, let alone say your goodbyes.

To leave your home under those circumstances, I know was terribly difficult. Not only the fear of the unknown, but also leaving those with whom you had a deep and long time friendship would have been most disconcerting. Fortunately, I have saved your letters, thus I have names of those whom you trust and those you do not.

My only difficulty was in getting someone to help me contact Thomas!

I literally had to camp on the doorstep of the newspaper building, waiting for the door to be opened to subscribers. On my first attempt, I was nearly in the employee's door when I was stopped by a security guard and was told I would have to wait at the front entrance. Needing to be at work on time, I left and returned the next morning fifteen minutes before the door was to be opened, thus being the first one in!

So at seven in the morning, I was on the street along with several transients, who kept asking for change or a cigarette. That was not much fun!

Once in the door, I requested to be seen by the managing editor, Roger Barnhill, and was told he was busy. When I said who I was, I received immediate attention and was taken to his office. Once there, I told him my story and he generously agreed to help. He inquired of Charles and asked that I give him his regards. I then gave Roger the message and the names of Brackham Wood residents of whom I thought you would approve. He assured me the message would go in the evening communiqué. Thomas responded with a telegram; thus I knew he had received my correspondence. I could only hope he would "keep the ball rolling;" an American saying from the election campaign of one of our former presidents, William Harrison. His supporters were encouraged to push a ball made of tin and leather from one campaign rally to another. Just think of all the American idioms you'll learn when you come to live here!

What fun it was to read your letter! Thomas outdid himself. I am glad that he did, as it made you so happy and undoubtedly made your friends in the village happy as well. I imagine you were striking in your Windsor Blue!

I am intrigued by your job and rather envious of all the interesting and formidable people you have and will meet in your position. How strange to run into both Robert and Malcolm. Does the fact that they were in the Home Office mean that they have been cleared of any suspicion?

Fashion has changed drastically! Women everywhere seem to be wearing high waist and wide-legged trousers. They look very comfortable and of course are appropriate for work in a factory. I think they might be great for leisure wear as well.

Charles' suits just hang in his closet; such lovely fabric. By the time he gets back home the cut of a man's suit will have changed. I'm tempted to refashion one of them for myself. I doubt that I can do it, but I know of a dressmaker who can.

Gillian has been back and forth between Spokane and Seattle several times since the beginning of summer. In June, the Boeing Company began hiring women from all over the country to help build airplanes for the war effort. The women have been dubbed, "Rosie the Riveter." The Federal Housing Administration has built barracks in which they can live. The buildings are near the center of Seattle's downtown. It's an area called The Denny Regrade (the regrade is a result of taking down and grading flat, Denny Hill, one of Seattle's seven hills).

Gillian's company builds wing components for Boeing's B-17's. It is not the building of the planes that has her going back and forth, but the fact that she's been serving as a security consultant. Boeing has also been hiring women as security officers and knew of Gillian because of Boeing's business connections with Brown Industries.

Dr. Barringer, the woman physician of whom I spoke in a recent letter, and her AMWA (American Women's Medical Association) committee have succeeded in lobbying Congress for military commissions for women physicians; in fact, this past April, the Sparkman Act, allowing female physicians to serve, was signed into law. Hooray!

Charles' training continues; there are no indications of an overseas assignment...yet. His division has been training in the northwest since September of last year. They are known as the "Timberwolf Division," because of their time in an area populated with the wolves. They are the first army division to train specifically for nighttime conditions. Soon the division will go elsewhere to participate in a combat exercise. I know very little about what he is doing. I am always relieved to get his letters, needless to say.

Bert will celebrate his birthday at the lake. We leave tomorrow for our month respite. He is quite excited as all three of the children have been taking swimming lessons again and he is anxious to show us what he is able to do. This will be the first opportunity in a year that he will be able to swim in water other than an indoor pool. I should have said all of us are excited to be leaving town for a time, even Gillian, though I wonder whether she will actually calm down enough to stay the entire time.

The children will, I hope, receive a grand surprise while we are at Newman. Charles has a week's leave due during the time we are there, though, by the time he gets to us it will be only five days before he will have to travel back to his division. If nothing happens to alter his leave, it will be a wonderful five days. I am not divulging the secret, as plans can change in an instant and then the children would be so disappointed.

My best to you, my darling sister, and please give my regards to Thomas as well.

With love,
Margaret

*****

October 30, 1943

My Dearest Margaret,

How happy I was to hear from you.

I was pleased to read of Thomas' part in our lovely ceremony and reception in Brackham Wood in May. The memories of that day remain as clear and as heartwarming today as they did then, despite how much has happened in the interim. It pleases me greatly to hear that my dear husband was an enthusiastic and effective participant in planning and executing that wonderful surprise. However, without your caring and initiative, I know that I would not carry that lovely memory with me. I am greatly touched whenever I think of you standing in the street in the early morning to gain access to the newspaper building.

You, my dear cousin, have a remarkable ability to focus on a future goal, identify and organize the needed resources and bring it into reality. I much admire you for this quality. I, on the other hand, seem to slide from one life circumstance to another without plan or predilection. However, at this time in my life I have neither the time nor the energy to reflect upon much at all.

Your comments on the changing lives of women give me hope that when our countries are once again at peace, women will be thought of more as people than as women. I cannot imagine myself, or any other of the women with whom I now work, returning to their prewar lives at home: fussing over the altar flowers or analyzing whose laundry is whiter as it hangs from the clothes pegs on the outdoor lines. Just think of Gillian going back to housekeeping as she did for your parents. And yet I cannot imagine how that will not be the case after the men turn in their uniforms and return to their former occupations.

Thinking of women working during war reminds me of how surprised I was to learn that Susan Brown, the woman who lived across the street from me in Brackham Wood and who rented her house to Robert Gentry after she moved in with her sister Clothilde to help with the farming in 1940, had been recruited for war work. She now lives near the small village of Milton Keynes and has not been home in three years. I cannot imagine what she would be doing for war work. During the years that she lived across the street from Michelsgrove, her main achievement was solving the Daily Telegraph crossword puzzle faster than anyone else in the village. I cannot imagine for what type of work that particular talent would be useful. Can you imagine what that would be?

Speaking of suits, I would encourage you to alter Charles' for your own use. Now that I have added two more to my wardrobe, I understand why men have always worn them. They make morning dressing easier and variety can be added by wearing them with different shirtwaists and scarves. The lined tweeds I wear cut the morning wind as I walk from the tube station to the Home Office building.

Another 'fashion' accessory that I wear is an identity bracelet. All civilians in London are encouraged to do so. With so many injured in the blitz, rescue workers can more easily identify those who are injured—and those who are killed. A sobering thought that.

My work has changed considerably since I last wrote. After a few weeks in reception, I was asked to fill in at several offices as openings occurred. I was totally overwhelmed for the first few days in each position. Some were so complex that I had no idea whether I was help or hindrance. Others I took to quite easily.

I was eventually called into a special meeting, arriving there with much trepidation, fearing that I would be sent packing. However, I was told something that amazed me. They felt that I had a gift for a certain type of filing. I shall try to explain to you what this means. There are many ways to arrange data so that it can be retrieved. For example, any meeting or event can be filed alphabetically, by date, by the name of the event, by geographical location, by code name, by group size, or by an infinite number of other descriptors.

My responsibility is to devise and implement a system whereby reports can be researched and generated in a variety of formats. This is a very messy process that may require hundreds of cards for each event. Would that there was some kind of mechanical device or giant brain that could simultaneously hold and cross reference information. You can imagine how much manpower it takes to handle so much information. In each instance, I write down the categories and others create and manipulate the files. Recently added categories, such as tide tables and phases of the moon add to the challenge.

I recently traveled to Edinburgh, Scotland, with one of my supervisors. While there, I worked 16-hour days doing this same type of work. The train trip north on the Flying Scotsman showed me parts of Britain that I have never imagined. Those 400 miles of varied terrain once again reminded me of how small my world has been. I am not alone in that. I have met several Londoners who have never set foot outside of the borough where they were born and others who have never left the city limits. Edinburgh is a beautiful city with the castle visible from every part of town.

While in the city, I worked in a cavernous room, doing the same type of sorting with different data. I had expected there to be much more activity on the streets, both civilian and military than I was able to observe.

Thomas and I are very lucky to snatch a few hours together on weekdays, partial days on Saturdays and all day on Sundays. While on a Sunday walk with Thomas in Regent's Park, I had a strange experience that I want to share with you. Perhaps you can give me some input. I noticed a woman wearing a suit very much like one that I had tailored for Harriet Malthorpe over four years ago. I had sewn three: one of worsted gabardine and two of Harris Tweed. The first tweed was cut from a gray fabric shot with red and blue threads and the second was fashioned of the same fabric in golden tones. The second is a much more unusual fabric so it caught my eye immediately when I saw it on a woman talking with a very ordinary looking man of about 50 years of age. However, the woman was a stone or two heavier than Harriet and rather than medium brown, her hair was jet black.

Perhaps she sensed my staring at her longer than normal because she turned toward me just as I pulled on Thomas' sleeve to direct his attention toward her. By the time he had turned his head in her direction, both the woman and the man she had been talking with had disappeared into thin air. Had they not done so, I would not have given this incident much thought. However, my suspicions were aroused and I have been thinking of the event ever since. Could it indeed have been Harriet? Hair color, of course, is easy to change or to cover with a wig or hairpiece of some type. As for the extra weight, she had asked me to cut the fabric large and leave more than ample seam allowances as I sewed.

Could this be a heavier Harriet or a Harriet secreting materials in her garments or did she sell the suit to someone else? I think that if I had seen her walk I could have answered that question. She had a very unique stride, different than the typical English woman.

My glimpses of Robert Gentry and Malcolm in the home office lobby lead me to conclude that they are, indeed, working in some aspect of intelligence or security. They had both been working for the government in other areas: Robert in supply and Malcolm in Inland Revenue, and I imagine that they would have been natural people to recruit. I still wonder, however, about Harriet. Perhaps she was in disguise and meeting with her handler. She may be doing the same work that we suppose George and Malcolm to be doing. On the other hand, she may be what is called a 'double agent,' appearing to work for one side while actually sending important information to the other.

At first, during the air war, information about weather, RAF bases, and the habits of the English, would have been helpful to the Germans as they planned their raids and strategic bombing. Now that they have suffered defeat upon defeat, I wonder what information they would be seeking. From the windows of the Flying Scotsman, I could see many roads and much movement of military trucks and guns. As we headed north, the number of military vehicles diminished sharply.

The number of Canadian and American soldiers on the streets of London seems to grow from weekend to weekend. I imagine that the Germans suspect an invasion. They keep fighting on even though they have lost much. Italy surrendered to the Allies on September 8, and declared war on Germany on October 13. Yet, fighting continues on Italian soil. Nazi Germany has begun to evacuate civilians from Berlin. With their forces diminished and diffused it would be impossible to defend the entire French coast. Therefore, they no doubt need information on where troops are mustering.

We here in Britain hear rumors about possible sites to launch the invasion. Though we are quite good about 'keeping mum' as advised by the posters, suspected launching sites range from Scotland to the southern tip of our island. We guard against becoming too optimistic for a quick end of the war. Yet I hope and pray that this war is soon over, that Charles need never leave for a combat zone, that we suffer no more damage from German bombs, and that we are soon together.

Love to all,
Moira

*****

November 27, 1943

My Dearest Moira,
I can only imagine what it must have been like for you to travel by train so far from everything that you have always known. London is now your home;

that which once seemed so daunting, is no longer so. But Edinburgh, 16 hour work days, and the type of work that you now perform pales in comparison to the work which once occupied your days in Brackham Wood.

Now your days are long and tedious, but undoubtedly very important to the war effort. Some day in the not too distant future, the work may be replaced by the "giant mechanical brain" to which you likened the efforts of so many in your detail. Finally, you are able to use that wonderful brain of yours for something well beyond cleaning another's house!

I don't remember a thing about Milton Keynes. Is it near London? Mrs. Brown's war work is definitely puzzling. But the fact that she can solve crossword puzzles so quickly, may actually be a clue to solving what it is that she does. It still doesn't explain why she does it in Milton Keynes? Surely its citizens must know what is taking place in their own village!

I am not a crossword aficionado, but I suppose crossword puzzles are rather like coded messages. I have read that the British crosswords are much more difficult than those we see printed in our newspapers. The British cryptic puzzles certainly stretch the brain! Our puzzles have no rules to follow in order to solve the crossword like yours do. The article I read said that, in the British puzzles, there are many "code words" or "indicators" that have a special meaning in the cryptic crossword context. Learning these, or being able to spot them, is a useful and necessary part of becoming a skilled cryptic crossword solver. Perhaps Mrs. Brown is putting her cryptic crossword skills to use in code-breaking?

Harriet could be in London?! How intriguing! Indeed, hair certainly can be dyed and a seeming weight gain, in a suit too large to begin with, would be easy to effect. I think that you recognized this woman, initially, because you recognized the suit. After all, it was sewn by you. Meeting her eye-to-eye gives me chills! I truly doubt that the suit was in the possession of any woman other than Harriet. I wonder what has become of George Malthorpe and just who the gray-haired gentleman with whom you saw the Harriet look-alike could be. Robert, Harriet, Malcolm—all in the same place, at the same time, and all suspect. It makes me so anxious for you and Thomas!

Charles was able to surprise the children, and we did have a wonderful time at the lake last summer. But it all seems so long ago; and yet four months have passed so quickly and we are on our way to the countdown to Christmas! I haven't heard from Charles for over two and a half months. I do believe he is only a few hundred miles away. He writes when he is able, but his Division began participating in what is known as the "Oregon Maneuver" in mid-September, making it difficult to get word to me. It is the largest training event ever in the Pacific Northwest. It involves 100,000 troops and the "battles" cover over 10,000 square miles of central Oregon. The land in that part of Oregon can be very cold. It is rugged and mountainous.

Two forces are tasked with different objectives. Although they oppose one another, both are reputed to have excelled at what was expected of them. Civilians who live or travel in the area were warned that they would be subject to troop movements and unexpected detours. In early November, the exercise concluded and the Army began to repair the roads damaged by tanks and other heavy equipment.

We are hoping to have Charles home on leave for Christmas. I suspect that his training is almost complete and that perhaps this may be our last Christmas together for some time; although it seems as if every day the newspaper reports another U-boat has been sunk. Does that mean the end of the war could be near?

My workload seems to increase every week. There are so many troops being brought to Baxter General for therapy and care. It is heart-wrenching; so many of them will never be whole; mentally or physically. Without the Red Cross volunteers, I can't imagine how we could handle the care of so many. The volunteers are no longer just knitting and wrapping bandages. Some of the women have special training as emergency drivers. Many have training as a home or emergency nurse which includes actually practicing in Spokane hospitals. A blood bank for emergency transfusions has been established. A recent newspaper article indicated that there are an estimated 7,000 first aid trained volunteers in the city.

Several months ago, Haruki tried to enlist and found that he had been classified "4C," an "enemy alien," by his draft board. That is amazing as he is neither an enemy, nor an alien, but an American-born citizen. After several more attempts, he was just notified that he will get his chance to serve his country. The Army has formed an all-Japanese unit, with white officers, to serve in Europe. He will be with the 442nd Regimental Combat Team. Of course,

Yoshi is very concerned, but that is the story of all families who have service members going into harm's way.

Yoshi is managing to keep herself very busy. Between her caring for us, her work at the grocery store, and now a new challenge, she has little time to be depressed.

Haruki and Yoshi have two young cousins—Keiko (who is seven) and Maemi (who is nine). The Nakamura girls had been living on a farm in Sprague, a farming community about forty miles from Spokane. Their family had lived in Seattle, but the parents were placed in Camp Harmony at the same time that Yoshi's parents were. The girls speak English and are very bright and sweet. Fortunately, the parents had sent the girls away just before the "roundup" of Japanese citizens. Keiko and Maemi haven't seen their mother or father for over a year. Sadly, they will never see them again; both committed suicide in the camp. For some Japanese, the lack of privacy and the internment is overwhelming and suicide is not an unusual result.

The girls have now come to live with Yoshi—with us that is. It is a good thing that we remodeled the attic a couple of years ago for Yoshi. There is also a small room that I used for sewing; it is now the girls' bedroom. Both girls are enrolled at Hutton School with Catherine and all five children seem to have adjusted to the situation.

We are not the only family in Spokane to take in Japanese. There is a lawyer in town who has taken in a family of seven!

In some neighborhoods, giving shelter has resulted in ugly harassment of the hosts and their guests. The existing Japanese community has even been reluctant to welcome the newcomers as they are afraid that their presence will cause the government to extend the evacuation order to Spokane. Thus far we have experienced nothing but tolerance.

Please be very careful and vigilant, Moira. Your work could put you at risk. Thomas should do the same!

We love you and pray for your continued safety!

Love,

Your sister Margaret

*****

January 20, 1944

My Dearest Margaret,

I am so happy to have your letter. You are constantly on my mind and I am always relieved when I see that an envelope in your handwriting has arrived. I force myself to remove my coat and hat and sit down before I slit it, however tempted I am to rip it open and read it on the spot.

You are right that my life right now is full of long days and hard work and also that it is so much more fulfilling than my days as a housemaid. When I reflect on my life from the time that I began writing you some seven years ago, I feel as though I am a different person. I do appreciate your perspective on my situation and your words of caution. I must, indeed, stay alert.

Your reflections are important to me as I scarcely have time to think of the changes in my life and the progress that has been made since we began our correspondence. I have begun to feel that we really belong there with you, and find myself lonesome for somewhere I have never been. While listening to the wireless I recently heard the phrase "memories from the future" and I have begun to feel that way.

Your taking in the Japanese children truly warms my heart. I think of it when I become downhearted and it reminds me that humanity can reign even in the most wretched circumstances. I imagine that Catherine being the only girl and the youngest in her family enjoys having two younger sisters with which to share her life.

How could one guess that Haruki would end up training in a Japanese combat team headed for Europe? I hope and pray that the war will end before either he or Charles needs to set foot in a combat zone. Like you, I am skeptical of the news that the Nazis are in decline.

I trust that Charles made it home for the holidays. I know that you made it a wonderful Christmas for the children in any case. Thank you so much for sending the beautiful cloth. What a perfect gift for two people who are attempting to set up a household in wartime. I cannot describe how it has improved the aesthetics of our flat.

We set our two chairs at an angle and can now sit comfortably of an evening engaging in conversation and reading. With your cloth on the table we feel like royalty as we drink our tea, coffee, or Bovril. And for a few minutes everything is tickety boo, an expression that makes Thomas laugh every time he hears it. We have learned to appreciate the small things in life, such as the return of the sound of church bells last April. As we sit together, I experience a sense of family I have not experienced for over 20 years: cozy and loved and perfectly content.

You asked about Milton Keynes. It is a very small village approximately 50 miles NNW of London. I know of it because I have read about it. It has been a place of human habitation since around 2000 BC. Flint tools from the Middle Stone Age have also been discovered nearby as well as a huge Bronze Age treasure trove. It is a rather unremarkable village at this time.

I have a difficult time imagining what Charles could be doing. It certainly sounds like war practice. Can there be such a large area that is not inhabited? We hear of strange maneuvers here as well. It is very hard to get anything from the newspapers but we make assumptions from things we hear. Patricia Dimblebey now has the welcome help of her sister, who has come to live in Brackham Wood. She was forced to leave her home when the entire area where she lives was taken over by the military for a very hush-hush reason.

The BBC has been pleading for pictures of France taken on prewar holidays for an exhibition they are preparing. Our neighbor on the same floor has contributed a large box of pictures taken by the seaside. When she was a child, her family had taken pictures each year when they visited their French grandparents.

Never having been to France, I had no pictures. In fact, we who lived as close to the coast as Brackham Wood were forbidden to take pictures once the war began. Air Raid wardens confiscated the cameras of those caught using them. This applied even to pictures taken of children in their own back gardens. An entire generation will grow up without images of their childhood save those they carry in their minds.

Though we do not speak of it, we on the ground continue to see troops massing. I cannot believe that the Germans do not know of this. The only question in their minds must be the location, they are certainly unable to fortify the entire French coast.

I recently was sent to Brent, a part of London that I had only seen on the map. The journey was very unsettling because of the number of bombed out buildings we glimpsed through the windows of our motorcar. Of course, during my daily commute to work I pass many cleared lots and scarred walls but I have become inured to them. The journey to Brent reminded me once again of the scope of destruction.

I must confess that I have been very depressed since then. I have an eerie feeling that as soon as Herr Hitler has time, he will once again direct his attentions our way.

There is no past or future during wartime—only the present. The immediacy of war makes the past irrelevant and the future too frightening to imagine. There are daily uncertainties and constant reminders from coworkers who have lost a loved one and who barely have time to grieve. If one is to live through wartime one must learn to not think too much but to enjoy the present moment.

***

Letter continued on February 29, 1944

***

Oh, dear Margaret, the writing of this letter was interrupted and I now must continue. Please make sure that you are sitting before you read what I am to write.

We had expected our anniversary to be a day of joy and happiness and planned a little celebration to mark our successful year of marriage. However, this was very much the opposite of what actually occurred. I had been feeling unwell in the mornings for over two weeks. But after an early morning cup of tea and a biscuit I was ready to go to work and was not much troubled for the rest of the day. I thought little of it because one never knows exactly what one is eating at the Home Office cafeteria and I had thought that perhaps I had come upon some tainted meat. But then came the signal that the touchy stomach had come from something else entirely and the doctor confirmed that I had been with child for a little over a month before it died and passed from my body. Both Thomas and I were shocked by the realization, because we had carefully planned for that to not happen.

Only to you can I write of my grief. Nearly all of my coworkers have lost someone to the war whether it be a brother, child, sibling, neighbor, spouse, or even the grocer down the street. I have experienced these vicarious losses and thought that I understood but I could never have imagined the depth of grief into which I would fall.

Thomas and I both knew that we were rather long in the tooth to become parents and had decided not to do so. Therefore, I am entirely shocked at how painful is the loss of a child I didn't even know I had. The event happened on a Monday and I did not return to work for the rest of that week. Thomas somehow got his hand on extra ration coupons and cooked me much beef to help build back my blood. There was a great deal lost. I am still not up to full power.

I suppose that I am grateful for the essential nature of my work. I have always felt my work to be important. Beginning as young as I did, I have always felt essential. I was needed to keep the households of my employers going. There were clothes to wash, mouths to feed, and the children to tend. As my situations became less demanding, I began to plan my future and I felt essential to the success of my imaginary bookshop. Not until I worked for the Malthorpes did I have time to ruminate about life at which time I began trying to ferret out what was really going on. After this loss, my certainty about what is essential and important is shaken.

Dr. Monkslip made it quite clear to me that at my age, and after this event, there is little to no chance of it happening again. So now I grieve for the children that I will never have even though I did not know that I wanted them. I feel as though my heart has been crushed by a piano falling from the top floor of this block of flats.

Thomas himself has become much more quiet. I imagine that he too is suffering—experiencing the loss at a deep level. Like me, he never intended such a thing to occur. He is very considerate and has told me that he is happy that I was trained to keep a stiff upper lip. Not until now have I truly understood the cost of keeping that upper lip steady. My mind goes back to Janet Millican returning to the WVS shop in Brackham Wood after her son, Harold, had been dead but a week.

Scarcely anyone outside of Thomas and I knows of this loss, which perhaps does not matter We British do not speak of such private things to others unless we know them well. Is silent sorrow easier to bear than that which brings out public mourning? Would it be better to walk behind the carriage that carries my child and is drawn by horses with braided black manes? I do not know the answer to that question. All that I know is that this is sorrow enough. None of our pert phrases like "he/she is in the hands of our Lord" or "it was meant to be" comfort me in the least. To others suffering so greatly, maimed and scarred and lacking limbs, this may seem like a small issue; however, not to me.

I hope that you are not greatly troubled by my imposing such an emotional burden upon you but I am so grateful, my sister and cousin, that I can write to you in such an open and emotional way. Putting these feelings into words has helped me immensely. Please take care of yourself and your family. I need you all.

Love,

Moira

*****

March 20, 1944

My Dearest Moira,

I am so very sorry to learn of your sadness. You are the strongest person I know. If anyone can make it through this devastating time it is you! I am very glad that you feel comfortable telling me of your loss. I will try to be of help in carrying this burden in any manner you determine. I am convinced that getting your feelings into the open will speed the healing process.

It is very natural for both of you to feel the way you do. Thomas's innate sensitivity, as well as "what is expected of a man," is manifesting itself in the quiet demeanor you have described. We do not expect our men to be thus, so we are mystified when they become so. You have been able to understand his sadness; please find a way to discuss your feelings with him. I believe that when you are able to comfort each other, you both will begin to heal.

Dr. Monkslip may be a fine general practitioner, but if he is not a specialist in the field of obstetrics, then he is not in a position to cite medical expertise in this area. If you and Thomas wish to have children, then you owe it to yourselves to consult with a doctor in the United States who has specialty training in obstetrics. I will find one for you, and rest assured, he will see you as soon as you are settled here. Until you know for certain that there is reason for you never to conceive again, you must not give up hope.

In the meantime, my professional advice is that you should find a way to get more exercise— walking, for example will improve your strength and chase the blues. It is good to have work; it will keep your mind off your feelings; but it is all consuming at the moment and you need the exercise to balance your mind and body.

Enjoying your home, when you can be there (I love the conversation corner you have created), reading, or some other quiet pursuit you can do together will provide comfort to both of you.

Please encourage Thomas to also try to occupy himself with something that will provide him relaxation and a quieting of his soul. He loves to work with wood and as you now know is very capable. Perhaps, he can create another piece for your flat?

Charles was able to be with us for Christmas, but only from the Eve to the Twenty-seventh. We went to Mass at St. John's Cathedral on Christmas morning. The Christmas Eve was spent at home. The house was very festive with boughs of pine and cedar.

It was a full house! Yoshi, Maemi, and Keiko, Gillian and her fiancé David Stewart (they had announced their engagement the week before), our children, and the two of us.

With regard to Gillian and David: he is a Boeing engineer, who lives in Seattle. He is 15 years her senior, so will not be sent to war. David is a widower with two grown children. His son, Jack is in the Navy and is soon to deploy to parts unknown. He is currently stationed in San Diego, California. His daughter, Helen, lives in Portland, Oregon, where she teaches history at the University of Portland.

They have not announced a wedding date. I can't imagine what she will do about her house and her job here in Spokane. They seem to be very happy and not at all in a rush to make any decisions. Their reactions are so unlike every other engaged couple that I know.

I am uncertain as to what Charles' duties within his unit really are. When he describes them, it is in very general terms. The fact that the unit operates mainly at night leaves a wide berth for what they actually do. He says they will not be deployed, without further training, until at least August. I suspect that he may not be home on leave again.

Summer at the lake without him is unthinkable. I have not told the children my fears; it would serve only to upset them. We all look to recent victories as a sign that the war will soon end without his having to leave the country. Deep inside, I know that is not what is going to happen, but it gives me hope.

My work at Baxter is never completed. There is no end to wounded troops. Many of them are in need of extended convalescence. We don't have the space at Baxter General to keep them and at the same time accept the care for the recently injured.

Fort George Wright, which has been used for so many purposes during the last few years, has been converted into a convalescent care facility. It is a lovely space of late 1800s, red brick, three or four storied quarters spaced on a parade field that is bordered with lovely maple and oak trees. Among the many programs it has, one is very unusual: The 707th Army Air Corps Band recently moved to Fort

Wright. The band members, in addition to their military mission, now serve as volunteer instructors for the sick.

At first, the soldiers would merely visit the wards and play for the patients. Many of the patients responded positively to the music therapy. They asked to be given lessons. Now part of the soldier-bandsmen's duty is to teach the patients to play an instrument of their choice.

There are many other activities that serve to prepare the convalescing soldiers for life as civilians. Farming and airplane engine mechanics training are among them. The Army hauled in a B-17 in sections so the "students" could reassemble it!

Spring vacation is the middle of next month. I will have some time off then and plan to take all the children to the lake. They are old enough now to help to air out the cottage and clean out the winter cobwebs. If I can find a suitable renter, I will rent it again as in years past for the summer; with the exception of the last two weeks in August, of course.

If I can't find a renter, I plan to offer it to Fort George Wright to use as therapy excursions for the ambulatory patients. I have yet to broach the subject with the hospital commander, but it seems like a good idea and certainly we have enough property to accommodate day trips for a swim, picnic, and relaxation for ten or twelve patients at a time.

In Haruki's absence, Chip Silver, the boy he saved from the car accident, has been watching the place during the winter. Chip hasn't reported any unusual activity, so I don't expect that I will have difficulty in getting the cottage opened for the season.

Spring cannot be far away. It has been unseasonably warm and some of the daffodils are beginning to poke through the ground. I wonder whether it is the same for you in London. Do you see the signs of new growth amid the destruction?

I will keep you both in my thoughts and prayers and hope that your sadness passes with time and that the hope that it is not the end of a dream will help you move forward.

With love,

Your sister, Margaret

*****

May 10, 1944

My Dearest Margaret,

How happy I was to hear from you, particularly during these difficult times. You kindly asked how you could help. I must tell you that you have already provided me with much assistance and support by allowing me to share my innermost thoughts.

Your advice to begin walking is well taken. While I have very little energy or incentive to move, I have gradually begun to dismount from the bus a block or two earlier each day. It is a small step but one that still leaves me energy for my work, which most of the time is very demanding. I also notice that I can stay awake longer in the evening. On my last visit to Dr. Monkslip he found that my iron deficiency anemia, while still with me, is less severe.

We have learned to live on root vegetables and very little meat. The powdered eggs and SPAM sent by your country provide much needed protein and fats but iron rich foods are in short supply. I eat spinach and Swiss chard at every opportunity though neither are on my favorite foods list. However, they are not always available at our neighborhood greengrocer and neither Thomas nor I have the time to scour street markets.

You have also helped us both in another way. Your enlightened view of the possibility of our bearing children has provided an incentive for both Thomas and me to share our feelings about our recent loss and to consider the prospect of future children. These discussions have helped us greatly to begin to move on and have been a godsend, regardless of our eventual decision.

You are right that Dr. Monkslip is not a specialist. While he is one of the better general practitioners, the certificates on his wall indicate that he must be around 75 years of age. With our younger doctors all serving in uniform, our retired physicians have been called back into their surgeries to serve the civilian population. Of course, this comes as no surprise to you, who must be working all hours to tend those soldiers who have returned from battle.

I find it very interesting to hear Fort George Wright has been turned into a convalescent care facility. Including music in the rehabilitation of the injured is a wonderful idea. The American spirit constantly impresses me. Not only do the recuperating soldiers enjoy listening to music but also they ask for lessons. And then there is the fundraising for athletic equipment. I can only hope that such innovation and generosity will continue once this terrible war has ended.

Here in England some of the fine country houses are serving as hospital and rehabilitation centers as they did during the last war.

Your Christmas celebration sounds wonderful. Would that Charles could have had more time with you.

Yet I know that you organized a festive celebration for your rapidly expanding family, which, according to my count, has now reached ten in number without including Helen and Jack. Congratulations to Gillian. How wonderful that she and David found each other. Despite the songs, novels, and films about young love, mature love brings its own joy.

The signs of spring are welcomed heartily here in London as they are each year. For me they are particularly encouraging as I recover from this most difficult winter. Green sprouts give hope as they force themselves through the rubble of bombed out ruins.

The German army remains a force with which to be reckoned even though we now hear that young boys and old men are being recruited to fill in its ranks. The longer hours of daylight are also a blessing to us who walk in the darkened city after work. Full moons and clear skies help us navigate our way. This war certainly has made us very aware of the phases of the moon as we live without artificial light.

I have just returned from two very pleasant and yet strange and unusual work-related journeys. As I have written before, my work involves organizing information, most of it coming from radio transmissions, in such a way that it can be sorted by multiple topics. Most recently I have been working on an enormous amount of data generated by the forces massing in Edinburgh and the First U.S. Army Group, gathering in Kent and Sussex.

This adventure began the day I was summoned and escorted to an office in a part of this building that I have never entered, even though I have worked here for a nearly a year. My confidence deserted me as my escort opened the door to a most sumptuous office and signaled me to take a seat in an upholstered chair facing an enormous desk. I half expected to recognize the person who was to walk in. However, I had never before seen him or his image. He began by engaging me in casual conversation, asking me about my prewar life, family, etc. I began to relax once I realized that I was not being called upon the carpet for chastisement.

I am still uncertain as to why I was chosen for this special project but I have a suspicion that it was somehow related to my accent. In this country, ones accent is a marker of background and class. George Bernard Shaw wrote a play called "Pygmalion" in which the major character, who is an expert on linguistics, says: "It is impossible for an Englishman to open his mouth without making some other Englishman hate or despise him."

I was never aware that I spoke in two ways until after Thomas and I became friends. He occasionally says: "Oh, now you are speaking your 'toney' English." You and I had undoubtedly learned to speak like the other students at Charwell School for Girls. However, once I left school and went out as a maid-of-all-work, I spoke with a more normal accent; having soon learned that speaking with a higher class accent than one's peers caused as much derision as speaking with a lower. I was, however, appreciated for having good grammar and was often asked to help the children of my employers with their grammar lessons.

You may be curious as to the nature of the questions he asked me and what directions I was given. He asked about my work, how the data were being sorted, and also talked with me about my husband working for the American press. He then explained to me that I was to be sent on two motorcade tours. The first would be back to Scotland, this time by road rather than on the Flying Scotsman and the second to a location that would be disclosed as we left town. Each was to begin on a Monday and end on a Friday. I was to pack my professional clothing and personal necessities. I would be staying in hotels or inns each night.

I hesitated to ask what my duties would be but when he asked if there were questions, I plucked up my courage and did so. He explained that I would be accompanying a high official, whom I may or may not see who would be riding in the center car of a three-car motorcade. The lead car was to carry uniformed military personnel in an open military vehicle and I was to ride with others in the third and last car. While the official was in meetings I would be free to talk with the locals and was to answer truthfully any questions they ask about the scope of my work, our heavy data traffic, the hours I work, wartime London. Of course, I was not to divulge the subject of the wireless messages but could admit that they had to do with the massing of troops for a yet undetermined purpose scheduled for the middle of the summer. We were even given some pocket money in the event that we wanted to offer a drink to one of the new friends we were to make.

The second trip was to take us to Dover in Kent where I was to do the same thing and also, if asked, to also share that the First U.S. Army Group, commanded by General Patton was massing there.

Early in the morning, three weeks ago as I was preparing to leave for the week in Scotland, a messenger delivered an envelope marked "urgent" addressed to Thomas. He has received such messages before and each time they meant that he was to be ready to be picked up for a several day assignment within a half hour.

He prepared quickly as usual and we said goodbye. Minutes later, I left for Thames House where the motorcade was forming up. As I stepped into the third car, I saw three other people, one of whom was Thomas. He had been chosen as the member of the press to cover our movement through the countryside. I did not know what to say and took my cue from Thomas who gave me a big smile. Once we had set out and introductions began, we shared our story with the other two government employees and we all had a hearty laugh.

The second motorcade was identical to the first. We took over the roads with our three cars, each with banners flying on each side. Two motorcycles led the way and two followed behind. The middle car had shaded windows. People gaped as we drove through the towns and villages on the way to our destination. They stared intensely through the windows of our car, looking for someone famous. I admit that I more than once had an urge to wave. This motorcade took us through more populated areas than the first. Both journeys were a lark. We are accustomed to working so hard for such long hours that this was a very nice break. At each stop, our every need was anticipated. Our job was to spend much of our time in local pubs, restaurants and teashops and to talk to the locals whenever possible.

On the last day in a Dover teashop, I excused myself from the table for a few minutes. While I was away, a woman wearing one of the suits I had sewn had joined the group. When I returned I was shocked. Harriet was sitting there chatting as sociably as I had ever seen her. She recovered quite quickly when I rejoined my tablemates. However, it took a few minutes for the color to return to her face. She then addressed me as though I was an old friend. She listened intently as we chatted about the amount of wireless traffic we had been receiving and the First U.S. Army Group (FUSAG) commanded by General Patton. She seemed uncharacteristically interested in what I was saying but offered no explanation of why she was there.

Not one of us saw the celebrity who was riding in the central car. In fact, it may have been empty. It was always unloaded inside a secure area with a line of guards forming a wall to shield its occupant from view as he walked from the car until he was safely inside the building.

This was a very strange assignment, but the variety, rest, and good food helped me on my way to recovery. I can only conclude that the government wanted to make a great spectacle and to send out some loose-lipped employees to talk about these two very active sites where large numbers of troops were stationed.

Whatever we did, I hope and pray that it helped in some small way to bring an end to this terrible war. Then Charles can safely come home, Thomas and I can get on with our lives and we can all begin to rebuild and refresh.

I am hopeful.

Very much love,

Moira

*****

September 6, 1944

My Dearest Moira,

I am trying to remember when last I wrote; I think that it was in late April. Now it is September and I have yet to get a response to my letter.

I'm terribly worried. I tried to get some information from the newspaper here, thinking that

I could send a message to Thomas. Unlike before, I couldn't get anyone to respond to my inquiries; other than to say they had no confirmation that anything untoward had happened to Thomas.

There was no offer to even send a message. Despite my requests, I was told that they could no longer contact Thomas with civilian messages.

Then D-Day came and went, and yet not a word from you. The buzz bombs were the next report of terror raining down on London. Where are you and Thomas? Are you safe? I pray that this letter finds you well. I wonder if perhaps you never received my April letter.

I feel rather foolish telling you about my summer, when who knows what horrors you have witnessed. Nonetheless, I will give you my most current news and hope that your letter has just been lost somewhere in between. Perhaps you are wondering why *you* haven't heard from *me*.

I didn't rent the cottage in June as I had some work done to the foundation, the chimney repointed and the roof repaired.

I was able to rent it for the entire month of July to a single family. We were there during the last two weeks of August.

For the first week, Yoshi was with the children (all five of them) and I came in the evenings; the last week, I was able to spend the entire time in the sunshine with my darlings.

Our renter in July was none other than David Stewart! He and Gillian finally decided that they would marry and did so very quietly in Seattle in late June. They honeymooned at Newman Lake for the month of July and two more weeks in August. David's son and daughter visited and the children were invited the last week of July for a couple of days.

We were guests at the wedding along with his children, Helen and Jack. A few of Gillian and David's friends completed the guest list. Yoshi was invited, but there is still the possibility of internment, and of course she has the little girls to watch, so she remained in Spokane.

We took the "Empire Builder" on a Thursday night and arrived Friday morning. It was the first trip to Seattle for the children. After unpacking, I took them to a restaurant, called "Twin Teepees". David knows the owner, a Mr. Clark, who happened to be there the morning we came in for breakfast. He introduced us to the man running his kitchen, a Colonel Harlan Sanders. The children all thought that he was in the military and bold Catherine inquired as to why he wasn't with her father! We all had a chuckle, thank goodness, over her impertinence! We went from the restaurant to nearby Woodland Park Zoo for a couple of hours and then returned to the hotel to dress for dinner.

The wedding took place in the small, rather unfinished chapel in St. Mark's Cathedral on Saturday morning.

The Cathedral had been closed for almost two years during which time the Army had used it as an anti-aircraft gun training center.

The Episcopal Diocese had huge debts and had been foreclosed upon in 1941. Recently, the Diocese has been restructured and St Mark's reopened for worship. It sits on a lovely plot of land that overlooks downtown Seattle, Lake Union, and Puget Sound to its west.

After the ceremony, we went to the wedding breakfast at the Olympic Hotel in downtown Seattle. It was a long day for all of us and by five o'clock, when we boarded the train, I was glad that we were ticketed in a Pullman car.

Charles is gone and the void is next to unbearable. I thought after D-Day that he would not have to leave, but of course the war has yet to end. He was not able to be with us at the lake, nor did he have any leave before deploying. It is as if he has been torn from our lives.

We believe his Division sailed for Europe in late August. It is assumed that they landed somewhere in France. I have yet to hear anything from him. Has Thomas?

William is doing his best to be "the man" of the house in his father's absence. It is an abrupt and horrible way to have entered adulthood.

I am grateful for David's presence in our lives. He is very good to the boys and filled the immediate void during the summer. David and the boys built a bunkhouse at the back of the lake property. I had a slab poured in May, thinking I would have Ben and Chip Silver build the bunkhouse while we were there in August.

David changed my plans when he asked whether he could build it. This man has to be busy at all times, even on his honeymoon! Ben had ordered the materials and was happy to give some guidance, even though he had lost the contract. The structure is built of logs. There is no heat; three windows and a door complete the house. Inside there are three sets of bunk beds and a few open shelves. It's very rugged, but the children love it.

The week the children were invited to stay with the Stewarts, David had both boys involved with the project. Bert is strong enough that he is able to walk, albeit with a pronounced limp and a cane. He has become quite the chess player (David's influence). Catherine, on the other hand, has become very introverted—quiet and circumspect. I am worried about her more than I am worried about the boys. Now that they are all back in school, I am hoping that the diversion will be enough to keep all of them occupied rather than being worried about their father.

Gillian and David have decided to stay in Seattle at least until the war's end. I doubt that they will settle in Spokane.

She is keeping the Spokane house, for the time-being. It needs paint and plumbing work, which she is having done, in bits and pieces, in her absence. I suppose she may then sell it. It would be a wonderful home for you and Thomas. Perhaps Thomas will want to return to his former house. I will hold the dream of having you in Gillian's house as it is much closer to ours than his is!

Life seems to be quickly changing for women in this country, as I suppose it is in England. I recently read an article about the WAVES taking over jobs customarily done by men because the men were needed for sea duty. The article said, "...women can often times do these jobs better than the men". In the same newspaper edition there was an article about a Russian woman who is the only female fighter pilot in the Russian Air Corps. She commands a unit that flies night missions. Amazing!

It will most certainly be a time of change when the world is once again at peace.

As more male physicians return home, my contract at Baxter will likely not be renewed. With that in mind, I am considering other options, of which there are not many.

However, one possibility interests me greatly.

One of the doctors stationed at Baxter General, Larry Blanchard, has an uncle who has practiced in Spokane for decades. His uncle is also a surgeon, but being about 75, he no longer goes to the operating room. He is merely practicing general medicine to keep his practice viable for sale to Larry.

Larry plans to take the practice in an entirely different direction. His idea is to form, under one roof, a group of physicians each specializing in a different area of medicine. He is convinced that women will want to see a female general practitioner or obstetrician, rather than seeing a male, and is trying to interest me in coming to work in his group.

Although I do not have a specialty, my work at Baxter qualifies me to practice general medicine. I must admit that the plan is certainly attractive. The thought of working with a group, as I have been doing here at Baxter General, is very appealing. It would seem that a group, as Larry envisions, could give a patient the best possible care without his having to search for a specialist in a particular field. The concept works so well at Baxter General.

Without Charles to discuss my ideas, I feel rather at sea. I don't have to make an immediate decision, but by 1 January, I will know the status of my military contract and I may be forced into making a decision alone.

Thank you for listening to my thoughts.

I hope that this letter finds you healthy and safe and that the same is true for Thomas. You are in my daily thoughts and prayers. I want you both here in the safety and security of your family.

With love,
Margaret

*****

September 8, 1944

My Dearest Moira,

No sooner had I sent a letter to you on Wednesday, than your May letter arrived on Friday. It appeared that it had been opened, and it was somewhat scrunched. I wonder what tales it could tell of its almost four month journey from you to me. I also wonder whether someone else had read it before I got the chance, but then I read too much mystery!

Regardless of its travels, I am overjoyed to know that in May, you and Thomas were both well. Now I wait in anticipation of news, that after the summer months, you are still safe.

What a strange two weeks you had traveling to Edinburgh and Dover! The latter was obviously the strangest. It was wonderful that you could be in the company of Thomas all the time, but then to come face to face with Harriet? How in the world could she manage the situation? How did she explain who she was, where she had been and what her relationship was to you? Better yet, how could you even breathe? I hope you told her all sorts of "secrets" and gave away copious amounts of information. I'm certain that you did your job well, even if the entire time you had to hold your breath.

I can hardly wait to hear from you. Your adventures are much better than a Helen MacInnes mystery book!
With much love and relief,
Margaret

******

November 3, 1944

My Dearest, Dearest Margaret,

I am so very relieved to hear from you. I became very worried when the usual time between our letters had elapsed and I had not heard from you for seven months. That my letter had been opened should not have surprised me as it did. After years of correspondence I had been lulled into the belief that nothing would negatively impact our letters. I am now amazed that it arrived at your door at all. Where has it been? Who has read it and why? I do have some ideas.

Thomas has had no word of Charles but is not particularly concerned. He constantly tells me not to worry, that everything is fine, that the war will soon be over and that you and I will soon be sitting together in your parlor drinking American coffee and talking a mile a minute. He also said that when I get there I should use the term 'living room' rather than parlor.

Your letter has brought me much pleasure, and I implore you to continue to write me of your work, the children, and your day-to-day life. Hearing of you and your regular activities kindles in me the hope that one day my life will also be unmarked by fear, secrets, explosions, fires, rubble, alarms, the screech of missiles, and facing death daily. Your letter gives me the hope that this terrible war will soon end.

I regret that I am not there to encourage Catherine. She is just the right age to enjoy two person tea parties with delicious sweets and female conversation. How fortunate that David has entered your family and is serving as a male presence in the lives of William and Bert. I calculate that he must be around the same age as our fathers, were they still living.

Like you, I wonder about the life of women after the war. I cannot imagine what my post-war life would hold were I not planning to immigrate to your country and had I not married Thomas. My age and experience would prevent me from re-entering a maid-of-all work position. Damage to the economy and the infrastructure of this country would keep me from fulfilling my bookstore dream for at least a decade. The vision of reaching your doorstep has inspired me to continue even in my darkest hours of which there have lately been many.

Like you, I conclude that my journeys to Edinburgh and Dover were part of an effort to encourage the Germans to set up defensive positions opposite those areas. As we now know, the actual invasion took place on the Coast of Normandy. D-Day brought us much hope and joy. Yet, the war continues. My position at the Home Office is changing. With the end in sight, my workload is slowly dropping off and I am occasionally directed to fill in for absentees in other parts of the building. My work is also less demanding, which is a benefit to me as I deal with other parts of my life, which I must now share with you even though I know that they will bring you grief.

Nothing I have read of or experienced has prepared me for the past five months. We who live in the south of England should have known that D-Day was to be launched from here, given the numbers of lorries, guns, and other strange vehicles heading south. Patricia Dimblebey wrote that they were parked alongside the roads all over their immediate area. There seemed to be more than a million American soldiers on the streets of London alone. While I am quite good at understanding American English, some of them spoke a dialect that I could scarcely decipher.

Around 9:30 on the morning of June 6, a special BBC bulletin announced that D-Day had come. Winston Churchill delivered this news to the House of Commons at noon. Six hours later, he announced to them that the invasion had been an outstanding success with the Germans suffering 10,000 casualties, 3,000 of which were fatalities. He did not, however, announce how many Allied troops were lost and still has not done so. Surely men were lost on both sides.

Many cheered when they heard the news that day, certain that they would soon be pulling down their blackout curtains. That joy, however, was short lived and I now grow pessimistic; wondering if the war will ever end. At the beginning of June, we had nearly forgotten about danger from the air. However, just as we became adjusted to our situation, a new weapon was hurled at us. We had not seen German aircraft overhead for a long time even though both the RAF and the American Army Air Corps regularly crossed our skies. The country cheered when the wireless reported the successful bombings of large German cities. However, it was only a matter of time until the Germans began to strike back.

The summer just past was very grey and rainy. Storm after storm hit London. In addition to the bad weather, on June 13, one week after D Day, the first of the horrible Vergeltungswaffe (V-1) flying bombs began landing on our country. We refer to them as

'Doodlebugs' to make them seem less menacing. They are terrifying despite the clever moniker we gave them. These 'flying bombs' are more terrifying than the Blitz. Witnesses to the first attack heard a new sound that they could identify only as a motorcycle without a muffler and a sight that they thought was an aeroplane with its tail on fire. We soon learned that as long as you could hear the loud sound, you were safe. However, once the engine cut out, all within hearing distance were in grave danger. The deadly weapon hit ground 15 seconds later.

The blast waves that followed the initial impact, blew over and killed people walking down the street. During the Blitz, RAF fighters had taken to the air and downed many incoming German aircraft. However, using anti-aircraft fire against the new bombs quickly ceased because of the number of people killed on the ground.

The V-1s destroyed railroad crossings, churches, department stores, homes, monuments, and took many, many lives. We may never know the number. At first the British press reported very little of the damage from Doodlebugs, but of course I knew through Thomas and I must admit that I did panic. So unnerved did I become that we moved from Devonshire Street to what we thought would be a safer location. Little did I know that much worse was to come. We had no more than arranged our furniture before a V-1 dropped on our street. Although we were just outside the edge of the blast zone, a fire had been ignited. We grabbed our important possessions and ran until we could run no further.

Thankfully, Thomas had always insisted that we each keep a 'ready box' as he had advised me to do when I lived in Brackham Wood. Mine contained your letters, Aunt Elizabeth's handkerchief, one suit, 3 shirtwaists, underclothing and grooming items. Thomas' box contained similar clothing items, three books, writing supplies, two manuscripts, and his shaving kit. We were invited to shelter with two men who have an extra bedroom, a rather large lounge and a well-equipped kitchen.

I now spend most of my non-working hours resting and sleeping and trying to find myself underneath the turmoil in my mind. I think that Thomas very much enjoys the camaraderie of Maxwell and Michael, as I certainly am not good company.

The second of August was the worst day of the Doodlebug bombings. After that, the V-1 flying bombs tapered off, and once again we began to feel hopeful that war's end was near. Imagine the elation on September 7 when Home Secretary Herbert Morrison announced that the Battle of London was over. Hitler would surely surrender soon.

The very next day brought us knowledge of a much worse menace—the V-2. No clever nickname was given to this rocket. It made the air battle between the Luftwaffe and the RAF look benign. It even made the Doodlebugs look less threatening. V- 2s came completely without warning. No sound comes with them to warn of these giant missiles; they fly faster than the speed of sound. They appear before the sound of their motors. The first audible signal comes from the explosion itself. It is then too late to run for shelter. The explosion is followed by the sound of the motor and then comes the thundering boom in the air that could be heard all over London. We have learned to call them sonic booms. Ten days after its beginning the barrage stopped and we once again saw our English spirits rise.

However, on the third of October, an explosion in Wanstead signaled the resumption of the rocket attacks.

On the tenth of November, Winston Churchill finally publicly acknowledged that the attack existed. Only then was the press allowed to report on V-2 attacks. There seems to be no end to this cold, hungry, deadly year. The 'we are all in this together' spirit has now vanished and terror is the order of the day.

I hesitate to tell you of something that worries me even more than the V-1 and V-2 rockets, as I know it will cause you anxiety.

Harriet Malthorpe contacted me. She insisted with some urgency that she needed to talk with me. I have agreed to meet her for a late tea at the Lyon's Tea Shop nearest the Home Office. I know not what to expect but have made certain that Thomas will know exactly where I am. My only comfort is that he or someone he knows will be nearby. He questioned me at great length as to my motives for saying yes. A part of me wants to run while another part knows that I must see the matter through. Thomas understands but does not seem pleased.

I am mailing this letter to the U.S. in a different way and sincerely hope and pray that it reaches you unopened with no delay. I look forward to hearing from you soon. I enclose the address at the Home Office, which, just now is the best way to contact me.

Please give my love to all the family. I am most anxious to see you all.

Much love,
Moira

******

December 2, 1944

Dearest Moira,

Your letter was forwarded to me after it reached Thomas' office at the newspaper here in Spokane. It appears to have been unopened. I believe it wise to send future mail the same way. I will use the Home Office address and pray my mail reaches you.

Our papers are full of the terror you describe. Of course, the description is nothing compared to having to live through night after night in the fear that morning will not come. We, who live in this country, have suffered little compared to that of you and your countrymen. Of course, when our loved ones are maimed or lost, our suffering is the same.

This letter will probably not reach you before you meet Harriet for tea. I admit that I am worried sick at the prospect of what you propose to do, and most likely have already done. I am somewhat consoled knowing that Thomas approves the plan, although not pleased, and will be nearby. Why he approves is beyond me, however.

You were never one to give into complacency, so I suppose that you feel you must see this through to the bitter end. Why isn't it enough for you just to dodge the Vs, do your job in the Home Office, and come home at night?

You are so brave. I find no weakness in you! I detect frustration and weariness. I find that totally understandable.

I will not continue to fill these pages with disapproval. This needs to be resolved so that you can move into your future. You have become a different woman in the seven years since we found one another. I am so proud to be your sister.

Perhaps it is because life seems so fleeting that you feel compelled to meet with Harriet. I believe that you just want resolution. It is so like the young

Moira I remember; wanting to get to the end, avoiding tedium of the middle.

On a totally different subject, the radio, rather than reading, has become the popular pastime here. The radio provides news and programs, which the entire family can enjoy. Most recently we began listening to *The Adventures of Ozzie and Harriet.* The children love the stories about an ideal American family with two growing boys. Interestingly, the Nelsons (Ozzie and Harriet) are married in real life and to one another. They do have two young boys, who are not yet old enough to portray themselves on the show.

Perhaps *your* dream bookshop could offer something more than just books; you could serve tea and sandwiches or scones and coffee in a "parlor" of an old house. It would be a wonderful setting for a bookshop and a great way to rescue an historical building. Bert would be happy to help you stock the shelves, although I fear you would find him secreted away in a corner reading, instead of working! Hold onto your dream!

Thank you for your concern about Catherine. It is so hard for her, indeed all of us, not to have Charles here, let alone not to know his whereabouts, or even if he is still alive. Families can only guess at where their loved ones are. We suspect, but have nothing to substantiate our suspicions, that Charles' unit is in the Ardennes. It is difficult not being "regular Army," whose family members live on the Post and are therefore better informed. We get little or no news other than that from the papers.

There is no news of Haruki. Yoshi last heard from him in September and of course he could not say where he was. His 442nd Regimental Combat

Team is being hailed as the heroes of the rescue of some 200 troops from the 141st Infantry, which had been surrounded by the Germans somewhere near Bifontaine in southeastern France. The 442nd's was the third attempt to free the men and are reported to have taken heavy losses. Yoshi has not been notified of the loss of Haruki, but we do know that some of his team have been reported as POWs.

I suppose you know that President Roosevelt was elected for a fourth term. I fear that the fatigue he suffers from his paralysis is going to take him before he can complete his term. He looked very worn and weary in what few campaign photos appeared in print. I wonder whether he invoked censorship to avoid the press reporting on his failing health.

We will attempt to celebrate Christmas as we have in past years. I am hoping to have the week off before the twenty-fifth and during that time we will take a day for a snow-picnic at Newman Lake. Then we'll go to the Silver's to purchase a tree from their harvest. We will have to drive two cars, but David and Gillian (who will be here for the holidays) are more than willing to drive so that all the children, to include Yoshi and her cousins, can come. We have become quite the clan. When you and Thomas and Charles get here, we will be complete.

I have no news of what is to become of my contract at Baxter General, except to say that Larry is going ahead with his plans for a clinic and they include me. At the very least, I will have an opportunity to go back into a civilian practice, should my military contract not be renewed. By the end of January, I may be temporarily out of work. Being unemployed could last until the clinic is up and running. So I could have as many as six months

to twiddle my thumbs. Oh, how I wish you were
here!

All my love as I sit on pins and needles until your
next letter arrives,

Margaret

*****

*Margaret was not to receive an answer to the letter
she sent to Moira in December of 1944. In fact, she
heard nothing of her cousin and her cousin's husband,
Thomas, until early March of 1945.*

*Her contract at Baxter General Hospital was not
renewed. Her friend, Dr. Larry Blanchard, returned to
civilian life in February of 1945. He took over his
uncle's practice as planned and within two months, he
and two other physicians—a surgeon and a
pediatrician—were working on the remodeling of the
multi-specialty clinic of which he had spoken to
Margaret the year before. She was planning to join the
group in April upon completion of the clinic space.*

*Blanchard's uncle had practiced in a Tudor-styled
house near Sacred Heart Hospital for over forty years.
He and his family lived in the rooms on the second
floor. His practice had been on the first. While the
proximity to the hospital was ideal, the structure itself
needed much updating and took longer than expected.
It was September of 1945 before the first patients could
be seen.*

*By that time, Margaret had been without work for
over nine months, but she was anything but idle. She
spent time in the Women and Children's Clinic, the
scene of her first position following her residency, as a
volunteer. For the first time in her life, she was able to*

see her children off to school and greet them when they came home.

Charles was still in Europe. Occasionally the family received a letter from him, but the letters were always months old.

Having her mother's attention and presence improved Catherine's life and disposition. She followed her mother's example and also volunteered, after school, in the Clinic beside her mother. Catherine had read of a project, called Candy Stripers, initiated by some East Orange, New Jersey high school girls. The girls worked in a local hospital dressed in red and white striped uniforms, which they themselves had made. She was able to engage her mother's help in creating a red-and-white striped apron to wear on the days she volunteered. William would begin his last year of high school in September, while Bert would be a sophomore.

But I am getting ahead of myself. On March 4, 1945, Margaret and her children and Yoshi and her two cousins had just finished supper, when the doorbell rang. Upon answering it, Margaret came face to face with an Air Force Major and a hollow-eyed woman who remotely resembled herself. The major identified the woman as Moira Walker.

After moments of silent shock, the family sprang into action. It was William who first moved, offering his arm and leading his Aunt Moira into the nearest chair and settling a blanket around her. Bert went immediately to the kitchen and Catherine moved to Margaret's side. She had never seen her mother fail to react in a crisis. Once she had regained her voice, Margaret attempted to extract information from Major Smith. He could tell her only that he had been ordered to deliver his charge to W 207 14th Avenue in Spokane and remain with her until she was in safe hands, at which time he was to return immediately to the Moses Lake Army Air Base.

The major reported that Moira had arrived on a troop-transport flight at the Base three days earlier. He had little to report about the journey to Spokane, telling Margaret only that his charge had stared straight ahead during the entire 100-mile road trip. His attempts to engage her in conversation bore no fruit. His only success had been to entice her to drink water from a canteen that had been given to him when he began this mission.

Bert had the presence of mind to prepare tea for Margaret and Moira. He called for Catherine and the two of them delivered tea and the cookies that had been set aside for dessert. This was a moment that the family never tired of reliving in later years. The two women sat in armchairs silently sipping tea. Though it lasted only for a few minutes, to Margaret's children it seemed like hours until their mother began acting like herself.

As soon as William carried her medical bag into the room, she became the mother they knew. After taking Moira's vital signs, Margaret determined that no immediate medical intervention was needed. Then there began a flurry of activity. After a bed was stripped, remade with clean linen, and night clothing located, the children and Yoshi returned to their own activities and Margaret settled Moira in for the night.

With Moira settled in Charles' bed, Margaret began an all-night vigil. But soon, she too, was asleep as Moira didn't move from a tightly curled ball of sleep.

Rising to see the children off to school, Margaret cancelled her day's plans and began the wait, which in later years' reflection seemed to be forever. By noon, when Moira had yet to appear, Margaret returned to her bedside with a tea tray.

Moira was on her back staring at the ceiling. It appeared that she had been crying, but she continued her silence. Her face showed no emotion, just the tear stains.

Tea was the only communication the women would share together for several days. Moira would not leave the room, eating only a portion of the meals that were brought to her.

The children visited their aunt in the afternoon upon returning from school. They shared their day with her without response. Maemi and Keiko only watched silently from the doorway.

Yoshi prepared a bath each morning, which Moira understood had been drawn for her. Yoshi commented to Margaret on the condition of the room after Moira had returned to her bed, saying that the room became cleaner with every day's passing.

Margaret began to wonder whether Moira was actually making progress. No words had passed between the cousins, but occasionally there was something that Margaret thought might be the beginnings of a smile.

Eight days after Moira's appearance, there was a heavy snowfall. The children had been sent home early and school had been cancelled for the following day. The family's routine became skewed. The children slept a little longer, Yoshi and Margaret did as well. The house was silent but for the running of bathwater and the sound of the teakettle working toward a boil. When the family finally arose, Margaret found the bed next to her empty. She went through the house searching for Moira. Margaret found her in the window nook next to Maemi, who was curled up in a blanket with only her hands exposed. The little girl was holding Moira's hand.

Shocked by a sudden memory, Margaret fell into a nearby child's chair. She had always loved the window nook in this upstairs bedroom. Perhaps that is why she had bought this 'Heidi' house. This room had immediately become her sewing room and remained so until Maemi Nakamura and her younger sister Keiko came to live with the family after their parents had died.

In their few years together at the beginning of their lives, she and Moira had frequently spent the night together at one or other of their homes. The memory that began to stir in Margaret was of waking up early one morning after Moira had spent the night with her. They loved to sit together in the window nook in Margaret's room and look out at the birds in a nearby tree. One night they had wrapped themselves in blankets and had fallen asleep right in their viewing place. Margaret had awakened to find she was holding Moira's hand in much the same way that Maemi was now holding the hand of a much older Moira.

As the shock wore off, Margaret realized that was the first time that Moira had moved through the house on her own. She was afraid to predict that this would be the long awaited breakthrough, but she allowed herself to become a little encouraged. She wondered if Moira was reliving her childhood and, if so, how long would it take until she became herself again.

In the final analysis, it was a little of both—reliving her childhood and becoming a mother. As more time passed, Margaret could see a relationship growing between Maemi and Moira and soon that bond also included Keiko. Could these children become the children Moira and Thomas might never conceive?

With a child on either side, holding her hand, Moira would venture outside occasionally to watch the girls build a snowman or create snow angels in the yard. She could be found in the evening, reading to the girls, or showing them how to make clothes for their dolls.

When the weather warmed, Moira liked to spend time in the garden. The younger girls were eager to help turn over the soil and continued to spend hours, when they were not in school, in Moira's company.

The relationship between Margaret and Moira took more time. Margaret had her volunteer work and her own children, not to mention a new practice in the making—all of which took her away from her home and Moira. Their conversations were brief, cordial but always in the present.

Yet again, it was Moira herself who reached out as she had in 1937 when she sent the twenty-year- late letter to Margaret's parents.

A month or so after arriving at Margaret's door, there was a change in Moira that became obvious to the entire household. On that marvelous day, William was not at home, and Maemi, Keiko and Catherine were busy at the kitchen table with schoolwork. Yoshi was at her grocery store job. Bert's voice could be heard, but he was nowhere in sight.

As Margaret walked through the door, the scent of lemon and chocolate wafted through the house. Cookies cooled on racks. Margaret followed the sound of Bert's voice and found him on the living room floor beside Moira. The bookshelves, which were always in disarray, were no longer so. They had been polished to a gloss and the books themselves had been separated by content and alphabetized by author. Bert and Moira were flushed, laughing, and beaming.

Moira got to her feet and walked slowly toward Margaret. It was a memory that Bert would never forget. With the slightest twinkle in her eye, Moira said: "Lo, Ger." It took a long moment for the stunned Margaret to respond. Finally her eyes lit up; she dropped her purse and briefcase in the doorway and ran toward her cousin. They both began to laugh and continued until tears ran down both of their faces. Every time that Bert recounts the story, he admits that he feared that both his mother and auntie had lost their minds.

Just as Bert returned to the room with a box of tissues, the cousins fell onto the sofa, exhausted. Once they regained their breath, Margaret explained that when, in the distant past, their four parents got together they loved to recount family stories. One of the earliest occurred after Margaret and Moira were past their first birthdays and before they celebrated their second. As Moira and her parents, Reggie and Jane, walked into the home of Margaret, Basil and Elizabeth, Moira toddled right over to her cousin, held out her hand and said: "Lo, Ger" which, in her language was 'Hello, Margaret."

Beginning with this day of tearful laughter, Moira became a contributing member of the family; taking on more and more of the household duties. She was always careful to talk to Margaret before assuming a new responsibility. As a maid-of-all-work in England, she had learned well not to overstep her boundaries. Margaret does not remember turning down help at any juncture. She herself was struggling to find her place in the post-war medical community, which had been greatly affected by the return of doctors who had gone to war.

Moira had been with Margaret two weeks before she received Thomas' hastily scrawled note warning her of his wife's impending arrival. From that time on, their correspondence was brief with Margaret keeping him informed on Moira's condition and assuring him that all were anxious for his and Charles' return. Thomas' letters were under heavy censorship, but from them she was able to infer that Thomas knew of the event that had sent Moira to her in such haste.

Margaret had a thousand questions for Moira about the war in England, Harriet and George, Malcolm, Robert, and what had brought her to America in such a state. However, she knew from her work with shell-shocked soldiers at Baxter that the answers were to emerge slowly. Some were to come from Moira; some from Thomas; some came only years later as official British and American records were declassified. Some questions remain unanswered even as I write.

As I read and reread the letters between Moira and Margaret with the perspective of many years, I immediately realized that they, probably more than most people of the time, were aware of world events and, in most if not all cases, were correct in their assessments. Being aware of events on both sides of the Atlantic gave them both a broader perspective than those who were prisoners of only their own experience and press releases.

With the Allied troops marching into Berlin, Adolph Hitler committed suicide in his underground bunker on April 30, 1945. The German government surrendered on May 8, which came to be known as V-E (Victory in Europe) Day.

Once he had reported on the celebratory street parties, which were held on July 12, Thomas was on his way home. His first impression was that the town he had left over three years before was still whole. With its green lawns, manicured shrubs, undamaged buildings and streets, the contrast between Spokane and London could hardly have been greater.

He arrived at 207 W 14th Street to find that his sister-in-law had created a highly functioning household of eight people: herself, her own three children, her cousin and sister-in-law, Moira, as well as Yoshi, a Japanese woman and her two orphaned cousins, Maemi and Keiko. He was not surprised. Charles' wife, Margaret, had always been highly organized and efficient. However, after staying in the house only one night he realized that he needed to quickly find a home for himself and Moira.

He wanted to remain within walking distance of this family that had been of such help to his wife over the past four and a half months. Realizing the immensity of the task before him and the fact that the home he owned did not fit the bill, he planned to broach the subject the next morning. After breakfast he asked Margaret if she would linger for an extra cup of wonderful full-strength coffee.

Margaret handed him the solution before he asked the question: he and Moira could move into the home of Gillian and David just a few blocks away. The move would help all concerned. Margaret had already made the arrangements and, if he agreed, he could begin preparing the house immediately. He left the table somewhat dazed and with the keys to a fully furnished home in his hand. Within a week, the home was made ready but he and Moira did not move in alone.

Thomas watched carefully for glimpses of the woman he married. He saw very few save for the time she spent interacting with Maemi and Keiko. He soon realized that Moira needed to be with them and they with her. When he talked with Margaret about his plan, she smiled broadly. He knew that she had been holding the same thought, possibly from before his arrival.

Haruki had been listed as MIA and before long, Yoshi once again relapsed into deep depression. It became obvious that she was unable to care for herself, let alone care for Margaret's children and her own cousins. Yoshi's parents had not survived the war years. There was no one to whom she could turn for help. She became another casualty of the war. Margaret found placement for Yoshi in an institution where she could receive care.

What of the orphaned cousins? They were both excited about moving to the new home that Thomas and Moira had purchased from David and Gillian. They chose their rooms and were fully involved in preparing the home for their move.

It was not until Maemi and Keiko, Thomas and Moira were well established in their new home that Thomas and Moira began to talk about the accident that had sent her to Margaret in such a state. And by then Moira was beginning to remember the substance of her last conversation with Harriet. Moira talked about that incident little by little, day by day, revealing the facts one by one.

Thomas and one of his co-workers had been watching from outside the Lyon's Teashop nearest the Home Office in mid-London as the two women met within. The two men tried to be unobtrusive as they peered through large windows, which had been criss-crossed with tape to prevent them shattering upon impact, as Harriet and Moira talked seriously. Thomas watched a conversational cycle repeat itself several times. First Harriet would rant. Then Moira would protest.

When Moira initially walked into the teashop she found a highly agitated Harriet waiting for her. Harriet began talking in her forthright manner revealing that she was about to commit suicide and, before she did, she wanted to tell someone about herself. She revealed a story of espionage and counter-espionage. As Moira and Margaret had both hypothesized, she was not born with the name Harriet Blake. She had begun life as Maria Oldenberg. She was the daughter of an English mother and German father. After her parents passed away, Maria was sent to Institut Chateau Beau Claire in Switzerland. Though half English, she had been brought up in a very stern German environment.

The moment Maria arrived at the school, classmates told her that there was a girl, Harriet, who looked enough like her to be her twin. Maria and Harriet were immediately brought together. Both saw resemblances but neither of them thought they were like twins. Maria, whom Moira knew as Harriet Malthorpe, described herself as a person who preferred to be alone rather than with others. Therefore, she and the actual Harriet Blake never really bonded. Maria felt little emotion when Harriet's parents passed away in a tragic accident.

The girls had taken some classes together, one of which was taught by the German teacher Frau Grunewald, who spoke perfect English as well as German. Like Frau Grunewald, Maria spoke both languages perfectly. It was her teacher with whom Maria bonded.

When the newly orphaned Harriet passed away from an infection shortly before graduation, Frau Grunewald hatched a plan. With Maria's approval, the German teacher switched the identities of her two pupils. Harriet Blake was buried in Switzerland as

Maria and the real Maria Oldenburg began to answer to the name of Harriet Blake.

Frau Grunewald, a German Nationalist who had joined the Nazi Party in the 1920s, had a great influence on the new Harriet Blake. In 1931, after her graduation from the finishing school, Harriet began her training as a German spy.

Frau Grunewald, using the name Monica Graves, took the new Harriet Blake to England several times as part of her training. Harriet's ultimate test was the visit to her 'brother' Malcolm Blake. Their meeting was formal but congenial. He had not seen his sister since she was quite young. The tragic fire, which had burned the family records, turned out to be an unexpected boon. At age 20, Harriet moved permanently to England.

Malcolm Blake and George Malthorpe, who were co-workers in the Office of Inland Revenue, had joined Military Intelligence, Section 5 (MI5). Agents were needed on the south coast to be on guard for spies entering the country. With Malcolm's 'sister' returned to England and George Malthorpe inheriting the Haberdashery in the village of Brackham Wood in Sussex, Malcolm formulated the plan to recruit Harriet to MI5 and have them marry. George could return to his hometown with no alarms being raised. Villagers would find it to be a perfectly normal situation. Harriet agreed to take part in the scheme but made it perfectly clear that she had no intention of keeping house. Thus began the search for a maid-of-all work.

The search criteria included finding a woman to help with cooking and cleaning, who was known not to tell tales outside the house and who had no relatives to inquire about her situation. After a bit of research, George heard Moira's name mentioned by several *sources. When Harriet, George, and Moira moved into Michelsgrove, George's childhood home, all seemed perfectly normal.*

As the women continued to talk, Harriet confessed to Moira that she regretted that she cared for George Malthorpe as little as he cared for her and that living in the same house had been painful. She even intimated that it could possibly have been difficult for him as well; an amazingly sensitive statement coming from Harriet. She believed that given the choice neither of them would have ever married.

Harriet admitted that she had helped the Germans by signaling information on flying weather and troop movements. She also was in charge of a supply of booklets to be given to invading German troops and it was she who had hidden them once the invasion was cancelled.

Her assistance to the German government had ended abruptly in November of 1941 when Monica Graves, also known as Monika Grunwald and by then well known to British intelligence as a German spy, travelled to London. Her unexplained death, shortly after her attempt to contact Harriet, will never be officially explained.

Malcolm had long believed that Harriet worked not only for the British but also for German government. Harriet's violent reaction to Monica's arrival in England confirmed his suspicion. He presented Harriet with the option of turning into a British counter spy or being prosecuted as a German spy: a sure death sentence.

After her conversion, she continued to pass messages to the German government. However, from that time on, each message she sent contained enough truth to be accepted and enough deception to serve the purposes of the Allied forces.

Harriet was never to learn that virtually every German spy in England had been incarcerated, eliminated or turned into a double agent.

After listening to Harriet relate her entire story, Moira was rendered speechless for a time. The words came to her slowly. "You have served an important function. You will be protected by the English government after the war."

Despite Moira's attempts to restrain her, Harriet ran to the teashop door, threw it open, ran straight in front of a double-decker bus and was killed instantly. Moira had instinctively reached out to pull her back and when she did, was hit by a lorry coming from the opposite direction. Although Thomas was by her side almost immediately, he thought she was gone. It was his co-worker who discovered a pulse.

Moira was rushed to hospital where she remained until it was deemed safe for her to travel. Thomas saw her onto a military transport and scrawled the note to Margaret that did not arrive until Moira had been in her care for two weeks.

As Moira and Thomas talked more and more about the past, they determined that Robert Gentry most likely worked for Special Branch (sometimes referred to as Scotland Yard) and was probably investigating Moira as well as George and Harriet.

Moira herself was definitely under surveillance during her trips to London with Wills. Since signals were being sent from the south coast, anyone not under orders, who lived with a suspect, would become a person of interest. They were both sure that George and Harriet's visits with Aunt Jewell scheduled for the 20th

*of each month were, in reality, meetings with their MI5
controller.*

*After the war, George Malthorpe remained in
Brackham Wood and continued his daily schedule at
the haberdashery.*

*Moira kept up a correspondence with both Wills
Barrow and Patricia Dimblebey who wrote of the
privations that continued for years after the end of the
war. Even though rationing on many items ended,
supplies were so low that shopping became even more
difficult than during the war. In England, rationing of
food and meat continued until 1954. Moira and
Margaret sent packages to Wills and Patricia, always
making certain that each parcel weighed less than five
pounds, since gift packs of over that weight would be
deducted from that person's rations in order to keep
rationing equal for all citizens.*

*After Moira moved into her own home, she rapidly
gained back her strength and personality and she and
Margaret resumed their childhood closeness. It seemed
as though they talked for hours and hours every single
day. In their defense, I must report that there was much
to discuss as their five children grew up and chose their
life paths.*

*William followed the profession of his grandfather,
father and uncle and became a journalist. Bert followed
the footsteps of his mother and grandfather and joined
the medical profession, eventually becoming an
epidemiologist. And Catherine, dear Catherine, what
can I say of her? She followed her own footpath after
graduating from Wellesley College, one of the best
women's colleges in the nation. She has been a dancer,
decorator and a worker for women's causes.*

*Keiko and Maemi both finished college locally;
Keiko graduated from Eastern Washington College of*

Education and found much work as a translator in many places in the U.S. and abroad. Maemi attended Whitworth College, where she met her husband Max. They live happily near her mother and father and she willingly joins in on many of Margaret and Moira's frequent conversations.

Difficult as it is for me, I must write that Charles was killed during one of the last days of combat in World War II. With his death, I lost my brother and best friend in life. Margaret lost her husband, but not her will to move ahead.

Once their children were launched, the cousins traded roles. Moira, settled and content at home, constantly urges caution and dispenses mountains of advice to Margaret.

As of late, Margaret has begun to wonder whether there might be a world beyond Spokane. It would not surprise me to awaken one morning to find that she has packed her bag in preparation for some grand adventure.

Thomas Walker

The End

About the Authors

Rita Gard Seedorf is a retired academic who became reacquainted with her high school classmate, Margaret Verhoef, as they worked on planning their high school reunion. Together they soon began writing *Letters From Brackham Wood*. Besides academic publications, she has written articles on local history and is the author of *One Room Out West*, the story of a one-room schoolhouse and its students. She and her husband Marty live in Cheney Washington. They have a son and a daughter and two grandsons.

Margaret Albi Verhoef is a retired teacher and school librarian who became reacquainted with her high school classmate, Rita Seedorf, as they worked on planning their high school reunion. Together they soon began writing *Letters From Brackham Wood*. Margaret, the wife of a retired Army Dental Officer, developed her skills as a letter-writer during the years they were stationed from Alaska to Texas and New York to Washington State. She and her husband Doug have a daughter and a granddaughter and live with their schnauzer in Spokane, WA.

10122024R00150

Made in the USA
San Bernardino, CA
05 April 2014